The Backward House

AND OTHER STORIES

HEARTPATH BOOKS LLC

CONTENTS

WORK IT!

The low thrum of the helicopter in the distance stirs the young men scattered and stretched out beneath the thick canopy of pines. One by one, they sit up and stand, and begin wrapping the heavy flannel shirts or jackets used as pillows around their waists. They take a drink of water from a bottle if they have one and a bite of food if they have any, and stuff the rest in a pocket.

They had a good break but thought it might be longer, knowing that the pick-up crew had encountered the same rocky ridge that had stopped them the previous day, and required professional climbers to be brought in and take the line over the peak and down the other side, where they could pick it up again. The delay had been a few hours, but this break had been nothing like that, and they figured the company had flown in spare bags of equipment to keep them moving.

As the sound of the thrumming increases, a few guys step into the thin strip of clearing cut into the forest, surveyed straight and extending for miles. Gazing down the slash line to where it stretches to the rich green density of the valley below, they wait. The thrumming increases until the lime-green and yellow helicopter appears, glowing in the sun beneath them. The chopper continues to rise toward them until reaching eye level. The group moves to take cover. To the side is thick with tree limbs and trunks, and the debris of trees cut and dragged off to clear the slash line. It is an effort to get far enough away, but each finds a place.

The sound of the helicopter increases to a roar. A great wind catches in the tops of the trees and slowly descends in a thrashing and whipping of branches and debris. Just down the line, in the midst of the maelstrom, appears the carousel, as big as a wagon wheel, suspended from a lanyard and dangling the five orange bags that descend and spin lazily, banging against trees on both sides as they drift forward toward the orange X taped to the ground. The bags hesitate, then lower before touching down. One of the bags is released and rolls onto its side. Amidst the maelstrom, the carousel lifts slightly, then further, until released from the ground. The bags again spin as they drift forward and up, dragging all whipping and thrashing, until they clear the trees.

The crew hesitates until all motion has ceased, then steps back into the slash line to stare after the helicopter. The helicopter's flight can give them an indication of what is ahead —how far uphill and how steep? As the helicopter climbs, it is soon obscured by treetops.

It is time to get to work. They step to the bag and roll it upright, then unclip the bag at the top and lay flat the four corners, revealing the contents of jumbled equipment. The two guys responsible for laying the cable move in first and drag to the side the eighty or so pounds, coiled in loops and as big as a horse collar, and begin untying the short lengths of rope used to keep the cable in a circle, while the other guys work on untangling and sorting out the sets of geophones.

They are the layout half of a seismic crew exploring for oil in the Rocky Mountains. Their job is to lay out the cable in mostly a straight line, then diddle out and attach the strings of geophones to the cable, then stomp the head of the phones with a spike on the end into the ground or on a harder surface use the pickax one of them carries to chop a hole. When a proper length of the line has been laid, the "doghouse" with its recording equipment will be flown in, and the line dynamited, creating the vibrations to be recorded. Afterward, the equipment is picked up and bagged by the other half of the crew and leapfrogged by helicopter to the front.

The two guys who carry the cable will be first down the line. It is the reason they volunteered for the job. Not knowing each other before but having worked seismic, they knew carrying the cable meant being first to see new country, but more importantly, carrying the cable offered them a chance to control some of their day. If they worked hard and could separate themselves from the rest of the crew, they could take longer breaks waiting for the others to catch up. It was a way to divide the day, one break at a time.

They work together. The cable is heavy and awkward. The guy whose turn it is to carry positions the cable, then giving the word, lifts the thick coil with both hands and with the help of his partner, takes the open center over his head and onto his shoulder. His partner quickly unwraps a few loops to reduce weight. They are off. The goal is to get as much weight off as soon as possible. The guy carrying the cable walks at a quick pace. His partner stays close behind, first laying out the loops in his hands, then looping more coils off while keeping up with his partner.

The first stretch is important. The guy carrying the cable leans forward and drives his legs. Every step is a step closer. When he can't go any further, he stops and leans over to relieve the pressure on his shoulder, then stands straight up and breathes heavily. When his legs stop burning and his breath returns, he gathers himself before starting off again.

Working uphill, it can take four or five stops to get through a length of cable. Toward the end, the person carrying doesn't need his partner and can hold the cable on his shoulder with one hand and loop the coils off with the other.

The work continues—one bag after another. The day is still and quiet except for the walkie-talkie carried on a belt crackling with chatter. They get their breaks, but only to recover. The sound of the rest of the crew coming behind is signal to get moving. Each cable is a challenge. The one guy is older but still young; the other is taller but not big. In flatter terrain, the crew can lay out ten miles of line in a day, but in the mountains, three to four miles is good.

By afternoon, even in the shade the heat is finding them. And there are more stretches of sun. As they climb higher, the dense forest they had been working through breaks up into patches of scrub oak, squatty pines with spreading limbs, and stretches of bare rock. They can better see the rising hulk of mountain above and beyond that they could only get glimpses of before. They could never climb it, but haven't heard anything about climbers coming in, so they assume they will miss it. Still, the direction means that at least the bulk of their day will be uphill. There can be small ridges and valleys, but the trend is definitely upward. The path of the helicopter when it passes overhead confirms their impressions.

Sweat gets in their eyes, and they have tied handkerchiefs around their heads. The flannel shirts that had been around their waists are used as pads for their shoulders. And they could use some water; it has been a couple of hours since they reached a water station. The company should know that carrying the cable doesn't allow for backpacks or bottles, but what does the company care? They know they're only grunts, but the company doesn't have to be cruel!

The whole focus is on the end of the day. They have to get there. But how far? The shadows are getting longer, but there is still plenty of daylight. The company knows their pick-up location but isn't going to tell them, and they're not going to ask. This is the time of day they have to reach inside themselves. One stretch after another. Get the damn cable off!

Their best hope is that the line levels off, but the terrain gets even steeper. Soon, they are leaning over until their faces nearly touch their boots. Their runs are reduced to twenty yards. Their breath is an almost constant gasping. They grab onto roots and trunks to pull themselves up. Ahead, they see the line open and hope it could be a flattening, but when they reach the top, the direction only leads to another uphill.

It has to stop. This can't go on. When they do finally hear over the walkie that directions are being given for pickup, it is a relief, but they are at the front of the line and will be last. They have to keep going. They wish they knew how many bags were left so they could at least pace themselves.

Word from the pilot does come. Two more bags and the pickup site will be off to the right. And the terrain does level off some. They push hard to make sure they aren't late. Reaching the end, the guy carrying the cable throws the head down and collapses to the ground as if reaching a finish line. The other comes up and collapses next to him. They both roll on their backs, bringing their hands to their faces and gasping for breath.

They keep breathing. When their breathing settles, they sit. They can hear the helicopter in the distance and get to their feet. Walking in the direction indicated, they find an opening with a patch of flatter rock that has to be the place. They decide where best to take cover, walk to the edge of the trees, and flop back down in the shade.

Across the open space beyond them, the world opens to an expansive view. From high up, they look out across a great valley to another rocky ridge, glistening in golden sunlight and extending above a dense carpet of rich green. Beyond is pure blue sky. The sight is impressive. But they have seen plenty of mountains. What most has their attention is the growing sound of the helicopter. When the pilot calls over the walkie, they confirm they are in position.

The chopper moves in with a thunderous roar. The guys take cover. The chopper drifts into the opening, bringing with it the whipping of trees and flying debris. Coming to a stop over the landing sight, the chopper slowly descends, hovering a moment before completing its landing. The engine revs down, the blades reduce rotation, and the pilot gives the signal. The guys run head down to the helicopter and get in, one in back, the other in front. The pilot turns to them as they buckle up. "Guys get your ass kicked?" he yells over the sound and smiles broadly, with white teeth in the middle of a full beard with bushy dark hair beneath a ballcap and headset and sunglasses. The guys don't yet have their headsets on and simply nod.

With the guys secure, the chopper revs up and wobbles slightly as it lifts. The pilot continues in a slow and steady ascent. Reaching above the squatty trees, the rocky face of mountain they have been seeing for much of the day is completely exposed, glowing in the evening light. The pilot drifts the helicopter toward it. The rocky face is massive. Getting close, the chopper hovers, then slowly lifts. Rising against the granite, they inspect the deep cuts and fissures just beyond them, and take in the many colors of polished granite: copper and blue sparkling in the sun.

It is the end of the day. They are the last flight. It is understood that the pilot is taking advantage of an opportunity to give a little tour. When they reach the top of the rocky face and rise above, the pilot drifts the chopper over to the jagged ridge and follows along the peak just feet below. The magnitude of the mountain is stupendous. It has been here for eons; the power of heaving and erosion.

Reaching the end of the ridge, the mountain drops away as they float out into empty space. The chopper hovers suspended a moment before the pilot rolls it on its side, and they cascade down the mountain.

GUITAR MONSTER

I need to be clear about this. I'm not trying to solve anything, come up with any great conclusion, reach some understanding. In writing this down, I'm not trying to record anything for reference or future prosperity. In that sense, I am only sketching, the way I might sketch if I were thinking about some painting. But even the idea of sketching seems too much, as if working in a direction, toward some possible result. My only interest here is to reach the center of something, something I've experienced, something remarkable, at the core of what I have become. So I am more like doodling—the mindless exercise of simple reaction and response. Just the word doodling causes me to smile. It is in the spirit of what I am after. Yes, I am a doodler. There must be an army of us.

It isn't hard to remember the start of this whole monster thing. It was James coming home laughing. I had no idea what he was laughing about. I was upstairs when he burst through the door, and by the way he was laughing, I thought someone was with him, as if a joke had been told just before entering and their laughter carried them into the room. I took a moment to check myself in a mirror before coming down the stairs. But it was only James, leaning against the wall with his head tilted back, laughing. I realized then the laughing was for me. Then I was laughing. It's so strange to think that I could laugh like that and not even know what I was laughing about. But the laughter was definitely release. There had been some tension. Leaving for the audition, James had such little hope of finding someone.

James was anxious to talk. He said they were auditioning another guitarist when this guy came into the studio, and they directed him to set up in the back room. The player they were working with was decent enough, but after telling him they weren't ready to make a decision, he left, and the three members huddled together, giving their assessment. It was then they heard some rifting and feedback. They didn't pay much attention until the sound began to grow. The playing raced around. Soon the three of them got to their instruments and joined in on some wild back and forth. They could hardly believe what they were hearing. Finally, they had to go see. What they found, completely amazed them. The guy had two guitars, one on each arm, connected with straps and brackets so that he played with his hands and pressure from his arms and elbows, along with some crazy electronics. They had never seen anything like it. The sound was unworldly. What ensued was the wildest jam session James had ever been a part of.

What so amazed me was seeing James so amazed. I thought he knew everything about guitars. Imitating the guy, his eyes darted around, his arms shook, and his hands fluttered. He had experienced a revelation. The guy had to be some kind of genius. The problem was that James was lead guitar; they didn't need another lead guitarist, and the guy could play nothing else.

The days following were confusing. All James would say for sure is that he hardly knew anything himself. It is understandable that the guys wanted to keep what was happening under wraps, but James and I were partners; we were together. The more he withdrew, the more vehement I became. The images that come to mind are of James on the back porch smoking in the dark, and me upstairs in my room staring at paintings that no longer had meaning.

Yet all it took before he left for the gig was for me to truly wish him well, and all the distance between us collapsed into full embrace, and we laughed and shook our heads at our craziness. When Kristi picked me up, we were only anxious for the guys. It was the biggest gig of their life, with agents and producers showing up. Pulling up to Blues Magoo's, the place was already packed; word had got around. We felt forced to push past people we knew who were anxious to know something. We made our way to our seats. I felt a pressure rising, the air was electric.

Finally, the lights went down, and the opening act took the stage. They were young and earnest and reaching for something. They reminded me of what James must have been like, but also how far he had come. After the band finished, the space returned to empty, and anticipation gathered. I couldn't help but wonder what James was feeling. His whole life spread out before him. I felt the intensity inside. I threatened to vibrate.

Into that dark space came a lone note of guitar, simple and direct, followed by another. The notes hardly seemed capable against so much expanse, yet continued into a string of notes that gathered attention. A melody developed, rich and resonant, giving space and dimension. I knew it was James. A single light came up as he walked out on stage. He played slow and expressive. A landscape developed, the natural tension between expanse and sound, giving testimony to magnitude and emotion. James had found entry, was admitting and effusive, extended the tone, pushed in a direction.

I was thrilled for James. Had taken the next step. In our life together as artists, we had always challenged each other and leap-frogged along in our progress. So the challenge was also for me. I would have to find my way forward. It's all I ever wanted from us. It defined our love together.

Soon the curtain opened, revealing the two other members on bass and drums. It was just the three of them on stage. The crowd was willing to go along. The band always had a following. Coming together, the instruments were quick to connect and extend. They were excellent players, tight and strong, combining in rousing interplay. The music created a spectrum that offered adventure, was determined to move and thrill. One piece led to another.

At some point, a low humming appeared in the background. The band on stage gave no acknowledgment. Yet the sound continued to rise. Finally forced to admit the presence of something else, the band's reaction was to pick up its pace in an effort to ignore and stay separate.

The humming continued to expand, low and guttural. The sound reached the level of the music on stage and threatened to overtake it. The band's reaction was to turn their attention to the humming and combine their effort in an attempt to overwhelm.

But the other sound remained undeterred, as some unalterable force, oblivious and constant. A sense of panic ensued as the instruments onstage increased their attack. A pressure expanded. The band escalated their effort in an all-out thrashing. It became a true test of wills.

The sound swelled to become deafening. Something had to give. The moment reached a crescendo. Unable to hold out any longer, and in a last-ditch attempt, the instruments abandoned their effort and raced away in all directions. The other music exploded. There is no other way to describe it. Sound screamed around me. My body felt pounded. The curtain rose and there stood the monster.

I will never forget my first sight of the monster. It was beyond anything I could have imagined. I lost all ability to comprehend. The monster was huge, at least ten feet tall, with a black spasming body, flailing and flashing guitar arms, lights shooting in all directions. What completely dominated my awareness was the head, staring fixed and impassive with red-beaming eyes, a face as much human as animal beneath flaming mohawk hair, riding above as some beacon or epicenter. My ability to process completely collapsed. I felt both captivated and condemned.

I have no idea how long it lasted. I felt transported and transfixed. At some point, words came marching directly from the monster. The words ignited a pathway, connected to feeling at some core in me, to a depth never conceived. The words kept coming, adding up to a swelling, until an equilibrium had been crossed, the words returning to fulfill a connection, the expression of relationship, as some activated volume of complete abandon.

Was I howling? People around me were howling. I was fucking howling!

I lost all sense of unity. I was unable to distinguish. I remember a feeling of both being suspended and having traveled a great distance. At some point, I returned to at least some awareness. Then I noticed a change in the space around me, in intensity and pressure. Staring at the monster for any indication, I saw the same beaming eyes, the flailing arms and spasming body, but the words had stopped. The real change, however, came when the eyes began to flicker. I felt a surge of uncertainty. The arms wavered; the body began to shrink. My reaction escalated toward panic. What I experienced most was a feeling of free fall, though not all at once, more as a slow and steady descending, as if the floor had opened, leaving a vacuous feeling in the pit of my stomach.

The monster's collapse continued. Its eyes flashed intermittently until completely extinguished, the arms sagged and then dropped to its side. The body settled to become a kind of pedestal upon which the head came to rest, staring out empty and lifeless like some dead icon.

The lights of the stage became dragged down as well, emanating only a low glow, illuminating a decimated landscape. I remember feeling exhausted, as if I, too, had collapsed. I felt abandoned, disconnected, stranded in some place, condemned only to witness.

Then into the void came the lone sound of guitar, frail and distant, as if wandering out amongst the devastation. It continued slow and tenuous, admitting but not dominating, giving testimony and assurance. The music gained space, gathered strength, returned air into the room. Establishing an equilibrium, the music drifted and faded itself, then was gone.

The expanse hovered suspended. I had no concept of where to begin; avoiding eye contact was essential. At some point, I felt forced to stand with the others, slowly make my way and shuffle out.

Out in the lobby, I had to reach James; it became the only thing that mattered. I needed to know if anything of us had survived. Receiving word that the band had already left, I knew just where to find him. Walking across that parking lot was the longest walk of my life. Reaching the far corner under the dim lights, I could see him smiling through the windshield and couldn't open the door fast enough, rush into his arms fully enough, feel our embrace. Then he was anxious to talk, as the combination of both our amazements. James said the show continued to develop right up until the last minute. He never even saw the head of the monster until the curtain opened. Overwhelmed, he kept his head down, playing for all he was worth. Back at our place that night, we came together as lovers suspended in a world we no longer understood. By the next morning, his phone was blowing up. It's no surprise the monster thing has become what it has.

When James calls from some other place, our words flit and flutter, tangled in space. It is the feeling we are after. We have lived and loved and touched deeply. What else can be done? The world has opened and we have given ourselves over. I feel power and expanse but nothing can be directed.

So where does that leave me? I feel lost to a life of sensation. Staring out the window, the world can be nothing but angles and shapes. When I eat breakfast, I am the person eating. When I talk with someone on the phone, I am the person talking. Alone in my room, I can't get beyond color and fill canvases with brightness and gloom. When I look in the mirror, my face so quickly gathers intensity that I have to look away.

This morning, I became intrigued by an orange, its peel with the spread of tiny pores like breathing skin. I felt mesmerized by the complex in search of the simple. The orange had grown out from itself in an ever-expanding bloom. Look what it had become! Inside, the sections seemed so brought together, and inside of each, a magnitude of minuscule sections pressed together like tiny teardrops, fleshy and swollen. Everything in this world breaks apart, but oh how it comes together!

THE LOVERS CIRCLE

A week before leaving for South Carolina, I received a travel brochure from the agency I used to book my flight. I thought the brochure a nice touch and contemplated how much the small gesture affected me to consider using the agency again when my attention was caught by the brochure's description of a place, which I had not considered to be much more than ordinary. The brochure described South Carolina in terms that were airy and tropical, with great sweeps of white sandy beaches, spreading flowers, and flocks of brightly colored birds.

Upon arriving, I found the brochure's descriptions to be surprisingly accurate. Driving from the airport, I noticed palm trees and blooming Magnolia. Rolling down the vehicle window, I was treated to a potpourri of scents, distinguished hints of lavender and citrus amongst the rich fragrance of earthy pine. Rounding a bend in the road, I looked out over a lushness as flagrantly green as the sky was blue.

Dropping my things at the hotel room, I drove the half

hour to the coast. Dominated by thoughts of wandering the fine line between sea and shore, I was anxious for expanse. But what I found wasn't at all the ocean I imagined. There was no shore, no line of demarcation. Instead, the ocean before me stopped and started in a series of inlets and small bays and was forced to fight for space against prolific vegetation; amongst the moss-covered oaks and squatty pines spread evergreen that would be impossible to penetrate. Though there were cottages interspersed amongst the foliage and along the edges of brackish lagoons, the feeling was that they were only camping out. I, too, felt dominated by the landscape and retreated to a small bridge over a thin estuary. I stood suspended between two great forces of sea and land, tangled in a forced embrace.

That evening, it began to rain. It has rained now for four straight days. The rain is incessant, deluging, a steady release of pressure with the momentum to overwhelm and wash away. So constant is the rain that people I came to work with who impress me as sturdy and resilient types are starting to complain. Yet I have come to like the rain, if only for its extreme. At any time of day, I can hear the rain on the roof of the building where I work, installing the Voice Data System I was contracted for. It is easy to imagine in the rush of rain, conversations through the lines, and I have found myself absently listening through the persistent rhythm to what could be a myriad of voices. At night, the rain leads me through a long draining of consciousness that, in the morning, leaves me dull but strangely vigorous.

But I am also pleased to find a core revealed. And at that core is a woman who has touched me greatly. I am surprised to find her there, as much as I would be surprised to find anything that could survive distance, expectation, and the unending volume of oceans turning back into steady downpours.

All I can say is we were ready. Just our meeting is a tribute to the wonder of the world. She came to a place she had never been and made great effort to drive into the big city and follow difficult directions to be somewhere special, to celebrate a friend who had helped her through a difficult time. I hadn't been to the club in a couple of months and had come in the mood of extending myself, believing the club to be an atmosphere that could attract the kind of woman that would interest me. It didn't take half an hour. I saw her as she walked in: tall, striking, with a strong hint of sophistication. It was her friend I first made contact with in a pleasant exchange as she was standing at the bar ordering drinks. Afterward, I shared a brief glance and smile with the woman seated at the table, making it easier to ask her to dance. Walking to the floor, we found a rhythm to the music and became comfortable moving around each other.

There had to be a time for us to become familiar, a time punctuated with small smiles and meeting glances, then the tempo of the music changed, and we were in each other's arms. We moved gently together. Surely the relief of closeness after so much empty space made it easy to dance cheek to cheek. In the desire to make ourselves known, we talked in each other's ear: "The music feels good," "I love to sway." Our words delivered at a level of connection, coupled with the full feeling of our bodies matching perfectly.

So quickly we rushed to that special place between two people. I sat at her table, talked with her friend, but we were both anxious to return to the floor. Just that coming together, letting the music lift us, feeling our bodies close. The evening ended suddenly when her friend insisted that they make a meeting with other friends at another place. Too much had only started, but more importantly, she crossed a line, and when her friend wasn't looking, she reached forward with two quick kisses that were perfect as the extension of her feeling. So, when we did meet again the following weekend, it was easy to move forward with smiles and a quick kiss to bridge our separation.

We met at a movie theater. She looked magnificent—lovely and radiant. Sitting next to each other in the dark, our hands continued their special language of skin as our fingers circled and entwined. When we did go to a club, we were again anxious to feel that swirl of motion cheek to cheek. Having given ourselves over to a rising intimacy, we were lovers already and were surprised at how big it could be.

She had lived a more traditional past, had a daughter, a business career, but had turned to social work as a call to something more human. I made a life out of staring at the horizon and chasing whiffs of wonder in pursuit of an artist's dream, yet as I heard myself tell my story, I sounded more restless than I ever imagined. We both had recent divorces and spoke candidly about the pain. She talked of being asleep for years and the struggle to regain her life, and when tears came, she let them be. I, who felt I had married for all the right reasons, talked of a depth of chaos and how I was still overcome with surges of grief. When the music started again, we danced to advance our closeness, and later in a dark car with open mouths and deep searching tongues. The power swelled so pure and strong it would have been right to go home together.

Even though we met several times, sometimes for lunch, all my favorite images of her are at night, dominated by the refracted and muted light of clubs, the dim light of theaters. When I picture her, I see her from the side, her head tilted back, her lovely face smiling wide with bright teeth and closed eyes, and I hear her rich laughter of pure delight. When we did come together as lovers, we embraced in the spirit of release and raced easily to the extent of pleasure.

If we had known we would spend just two nights together, we would have locked ourselves away. We knew of my approaching business trip and had already talked of the chance of her coming to visit, but we couldn't have expected her mother's illness. Rita had to leave immediately and stayed close to her mother's side. The worst was expected, but finally, she could be sure her mother would continue. There were the challenges of permanent care. All the while, she stayed strong and upright, and I felt impressed with her as being immensely capable. When she finally returned for one night to gather some things, I picked her up at the airport and drove straight to her place. There was no energy of desire between us as we left our clothes and lay in each other's arms. My role was to fortify, and I opened to the depths of myself and drew strength from all my life had been and could ever be. Lying next to her, I was aware of the rise and fall of oceans, the lives of kings and queens, and the great travels of men and women as they made their way across strange lands in search of rich but uncertain futures. This was our time. In the middle of the night, I held her close and stroked her body and breathed deep the scent I would try to remember. She reached for me, and in the morning, we made love as deep and affirming confirmation. That afternoon, she returned to what had become her immediate destiny.

We already knew the ineffectiveness of phone conversation to pursue a true intimacy, and e-mail wasn't available at her mother's place, so we thought to write. Aware of the limits of back and forth, and in an attempt to blur our separation, we took to writing notes. We wrote down quick impressions, knowing the other was doing the same, tried to capture wisps of poignancy and express sudden longings. Often the notes were no more than a phrase or two and could be a memory jar that could cause the room to tilt: "Remember the blue couch." "I love the place behind your ears." Soon, we were sending up to a dozen notes a day until a blizzard of notes filled the mailbox. I taped them to the mirror and then spread them across the wall. I wanted to be swarmed by them, immersed in their essence, as if pure volume could be enough. I have always been attracted to shrines, with their deep sense of mystery and pure devotion. My darling, I love you.

So my life spreads out, goes forward. Change is the great constant, and I have never been more certain that to stop is to be at least not rewarded. I feel Rita as a reference point of all that is alive and expanding, and feel desperate for us to continue. Yet I can't deny the possibility that we could end. What if we had our time and our lives were already shifting to different positions? My most persistent fear is that she might meet the man I will become.

Yesterday at dusk with the rain pouring down, I took off my shoes while sitting on the small balcony of my hotel room, and stretched my feet over the railing to be bathed in the stream of water overflowing from the roof. I thought of

Christ, having his feet washed by Mary, and the biblical implications of service and redemption. But I also wondered if, against his great dimension, he was able to fully give himself over to the simple pleasure of being touched by another, of having water poured over him, of having his feet dried with her hair. How could he not? Christ, more than anyone, was aware of the specific wonder of being human, the magnitude and mystery, and he honored that existence completely in a realm of love. How else could he, on the verge of his death, whisper those words of transcendence that will continue to reverberate for eons: "Forgive them Father, for they know not what they do."

Uncle Floyd

S tanding with others where he can watch passengers step
down the stairs and exit the bus, his first interest is to
be sure Corbin is even on the bus and has made the different
bus changes throughout the night. He then wonders how
much he will even recognize him; he assumes he will, but it
has been two years, and a lot can change in a teenager since
they were thirteen. But he does recognize him, as soon as he
appears in the door opening, the same flop of dark hair over
his forehead, the same quiet face that shows the spread of a
shy smile when their eyes meet. As he comes forward,
Corbin has definitely gotten taller; they come together in a
quick hug that is mostly the coming together of their coats.

"Well, you made it," he says, upbeat to say something, as
they step back from each other. "Must have been quite the
trip."

Corbin smiles in response. "Long," he says, lifting his
eyes and then dropping them in a show of exasperation. Yes,
fourteen hours on a bus could seem like an eternity.

They step aside from the others and then make their way

to the back of the bus, where the driver unloads luggage from an open bin along the bottom. "Get any sleep?" he decides to ask because he is actually curious about how rough the trip had been.

Corbin takes a moment to decide, "Yeah, some." He then moves in to grab his black suitcase, which is set out on the sidewalk. Standing it upright and extending the handle, he begins rolling it, following to the back of the bus and behind, before they cross the street into the parking lot. Reaching the truck, he opens the rear door and Corbin loads the suitcase into the back seat before entering the passenger side. Walking around to the other side, he gets in himself, and after starting the truck, backs out of the parking spot before easing out of the lot. Turning right, the road leads to the highway. Getting on, he brings the truck up to speed.

So there is the initial meeting. It went pretty much as could be expected. The big thing is Corbin made it. His impression of him is the same as he remembers: the same subdued manner, the same almost vacant stare as if nothing much registers; it's what was always a bit unnerving about the kid and what he hoped Corbin had outgrown. His next interest is to start a conversation before the space between them gets too large; he is the adult here; it's up to him. He picks something obvious; it comes from being aware of what Corbin's first impression must be as he looks out the window and sees everything covered in white. Corbin has seen snow before, but this is northern Wisconsin, a long way from southern Ohio. "Hope you like snow," he says, light and nonchalant.

"It's okay," Corbin answers, not so much giving his assessment as letting it be known snow doesn't bother him.

He gives a quick laugh, not so much making light of the comment but hinting at something more serious because snow is a big deal up here; how someone handles snow can easily determine a quality of life. The season so far hasn't been much with some decent snows but also periods of melt, yet things are just getting started; in an average year, snowfall can easily be a hundred and fifty inches. And by tomorrow, Corbin should get a better taste; it's not supposed to be a big blow, but a bit of a storm is forecast for overnight. "Any snow when you left?" he asks, staying on the subject, as maybe the easiest way to continue a conversation.

"Not much," comes back to him.

"You have a white Christmas?"

The question seems to catch Corbin off guard; he takes a moment to think, as if making a clear effort to be honest. "I think so," seems the best he can come up with.

He thinks so? It strikes him as odd. Christmas was just a few days ago, and having a white Christmas or not is such a differentiating factor for people; the quality of Christmas dependent on whether there was snow on the ground; the matching up to some sentimental ideal. That Corbin doesn't know is surely telling. A lot is going on with the kid; there are surely bigger issues in his life than whether there was snow on Christmas morning.

He wants to stay close to Corbin in conversation, to not let any serious distance develop between them that might be difficult to overcome. So he decides on a topic in common, something they both have feeling for. And he's genuinely interested in Corbin's opinion; he wants to take advantage of his firsthand knowledge.

"So, how's your grandma?" he asks directly, then glances

over for any reaction. For the moment, Corbin continues with his head turned, staring out the window.

"She's okay," he says, then does turn his head. He remains looking forward. "She has some good days."

Which means she also has some bad days. It's about what he got from conversations with his mother. And things are only going to get worse through the progression of her illness and the ramp-up of treatment.

Mom's illness is the reason she could no longer have Corbin live with her; it just wasn't fair; she didn't have the strength and energy to give the proper attention required of a teenager. There were no other good options. When the idea was first suggested that Corbin come live with him, he was quick to resist; his whole life would be upended, he had a lot going on, and he had no experience dealing with a teenager. But he came to believe it was absolutely best, a young kid was in crisis, his nephew. He's not sure how Corbin felt about the situation, he heard Corbin wasn't happy, which is understandable, being forced to leave everything he had ever known to travel what must seem like halfway across the country, to live with someone he hardly knew; but how far his displeasure went he has no idea. The real issue is whether Corbin might be harboring any resentment, maybe toward his grandma for all his upheaval and discontent; it's what he wants to address, he feels the need to set the record straight. His grandmother had nothing but his best interest at heart. "Your grandma loves you," he says into the space between them. The words seem to gather weight. Corbin's reaction is to look back out the window.

It brings up the other issue of abandonment, if only by proximity, the true source of pain, and he feels the need to address that issue as well. Corbin's mother is a good person; she always made him the center of her life, but she just got caught up in something beyond her. It happened so fast. His sister was a victim of the opioid crisis sweeping the nation; whole communities were dragged under. Being incarcerated as a repeat offender for fraud and theft probably saved her life. "Your mother loves you," he says into the center of what might be an expanding space of confusion and hurt. He says it in an attempt to establish a basis of understanding, but also as a measure of hope, as any chance for something to hold onto, maybe not even anytime soon, as counterbalance against what Corbin is going through, as a brick in a wall against any festering bad feeling.

The last twenty minutes of the drive are done mostly in silence. Reaching the town where he lives, he travels along roads to an outskirt area of homes on larger lots, interspersed among woods of mostly medium-sized, straight-trunk trees: dark poles against a white background. Pulling into the driveway, he parks in front of the garage. Getting out, he waits for Corbin to remove his suitcase from the backseat and drag it around before leading to the front door.

Entering the house, they both take off their coats and hang them on the wall rack. He leads down the short hall to the left with Corbin bringing his suitcase. Entering the second bedroom, he glances around, seeing it as Corbin will for the first time. The room is small, but no smaller than what he is used to, looks nice and clean with the well-made bed, a dresser, and a small table and chair. He has thought of adding a television and computer, but has decided to hold off until he is sure what Corbin needs. The most attractive feature of the room is the two good-sized windows located toward the corner, at right angles to each other from different walls, offering a good view and letting in plenty of natural light.

After Corbin parks his suitcase, he decides to give him time to get settled and moves past him back into the hall, then into the larger living area, past the couch and chair facing the television on the wall to the woodstove jutting from the corner. Opening the door to the stove, he stokes the fire. He is glad to have a moment to himself. Things with Corbin have gone about as well as could be hoped for, but it's still a challenge having to focus on someone. After finishing with the woodstove, he moves to the kitchen area, which is a continuation of the living area but smaller because of the intruding walls of the rest of the house. There is a dining table and chairs, and the desk and computer from what is now Corbin's room pushed into the far corner. Stepping to the countertop, he removes the crockpot lid and checks on the stew that isn't done but is planned on for dinner later.

With no idea when Corbin would have eaten last or what he might have eaten throughout the night, he had felt it best to plan on something for when he arrived. Without knowing what Corbin likes, he bought a couple of different sandwiches from the sub shop, along with two different kinds of small bags of chips and cans of soda. He puts out the food and brings a couple of plates and napkins. But before calling Corbin from the bedroom, he takes another moment to assess his situation because what he is up against is a big deal. He steps to the full length of glass door and looks out to the backyard of trees staggered apart, leading up the slope of the small hill that divides his property. The question is what he thinks of Corbin, because what he knows isn't much, which isn't much more than what he knew before today, so that he feels forced to rely on any new impressions. Overall, Corbin seems healthy enough, but the real story is what's happening beneath the surface. He has stayed aware, looking for some indication of bad attitude or repressed anger, but hasn't noticed any obvious signs; no piercings or tattoos or statement clothes—Corbin seems normal. He has a cell phone but doesn't seem dominated by it. "Hey Corbin, you care to eat?"

After another moment, Corbin walks out and takes a seat at the table. He offers him the choice of sandwiches, chips and soda, before taking the others for himself. They eat in silence. Afterward, he moves to the woodstove to adjust the heat.

The decision is what to do next. He doesn't have anything planned, having felt it best just to let the day unfold, take his cue from the kid, have him be considered. But nothing clear comes to mind. He is sure Corbin would be fine with going to his room and taking a nap, but if he fell asleep, he could wake with the night ahead, and maybe not be able to get back to sleep. The challenge is spending time together. He does have something in mind that needs to be done anyway, and it suddenly feels right. "Hey, how 'bout doing some grocery shopping?" He feels the need to explain. "I'll take care of dinners; you take care of breakfast and lunch. We'll get what you want." His idea is to make Corbin comfortable, get him involved, make him feel like he has a say in his living. The idea is linked to the understanding that food is a big part of being a teenager. It's also the chance to demonstrate that he is aware of him, that he cares, is being considerate. They walk to the door and put on their coats.

After the short drive to the grocery, he directs Corbin to take a cart from inside the door, and the two of them walk side-by-side to one end and start down the first of eight or so aisles that divide the store. He lets him take the lead, and as Corbin makes his selections, they become almost comical; typical stuff for a teenager: frosted cereal, boxes of mac-n-cheese, packaged bologna, a jar of peanut butter, jam, white bread—not even an attempt at eating healthy. What does get his attention is when Corbin chooses energy drinks over soda; soda is bad enough, but energy drinks worse; he decides to let it slide this time but it will be the last. Finished with shopping, they proceed through check-out before grabbing the bags of groceries and leaving the cart.

The trip to the grocery hasn't taken long; there is still plenty of afternoon left. With nothing else planned and no interest in returning home, he decides to give Corbin a tour of the town where he will be living. Driving Main Street, both sides are lined with small stores and shops, a bar, and a couple of restaurants that are all familiar, but nothing of great distinction and no real landmarks. The town is definitely smaller than the city Corbin came from. Beyond Main Street, there are only the small houses of the neighborhood.

He decides to make the short drive to the area's high school. It should be interesting for Corbin. This will be the center of his life, where Corbin will make new friends, spend much of his time; in the next day or so, he'll be taking him to sign up for classes. For now, the school is closed for the holiday break. He drives slowly down the full length of the building so Corbin can get a good look. It's a decent-sized school for a small town with kids drawn from the entire area. Even empty, the building appears stout and hulking with its gray-brick façade. Looking over at him, it is impossible to tell what Corbin is thinking; he seems to be taking it all in with his head turned, staring out the window.

Past the school, there are a few scattered homes but mostly open space. It still feels too early to drive home. Something else comes to mind, which comes from the idea of wanting to give Corbin a full picture of his new life. If he wants that view to be complete, he might as well include himself as part of the equation. His inclination is to take him to his shop in the light industrial area just outside of town and show him where he works. The shop is the culmination of so much effort, something he had been working toward for years—a key component to who he is, a source of much pride. But as he sits with the idea, it seems a bit much, too soon. His interest in giving Corbin a tour was to focus on what would be the features of his future, and showing him the woodworking shop would be a bit of a tangent, and probably a little self-serving. Instead, he comes up with another idea and turns the truck onto the road leading out of town. In no time, houses become more intermittent, and the size of fields and openings begin to diminish. Soon they travel through continuous trees, passing to either side in a steady stream.

The most distinguishing feature of the whole area is the expanse of forest. It is a thing Corbin will have to come to terms with. For some, the vastness of this place is a source of enjoyment and inspiration, himself included, but for others, a source of isolation that compounds a feeling of limitation and dismay. They have entered a national forest; it goes on and on. It is the feeling he wants Corbin to have, the feeling of bigness, of vast and open space; it adds up to become a volume of nature, something substantial, a sense of what is beyond, but more importantly something he can connect to if he wants, as a place to draw strength. In that sense, he will leave it up to Corbin to decide what he thinks; his interest now is just to present him to the wild.

But after a while, the attempt feels a bit heavy-handed, as if driving him out here without reason or explanation might be felt as imposing or even a little weird; he has no idea what Corbin could be thinking. And his reasoning would be hard to explain, the real truth that he is doing this for him, in the hope of giving perspective, that Corbin might be aware of a world beyond himself, that he will open to possibility. He decides on another approach, as something to lead toward another truth, or at least something with an element of truth, as a partial explanation. "You know I'm a woodworker," he starts. Of the little Corbin knows about him, he is sure Corbin knows he makes his living installing cabinets and building furniture. "I like looking at trees." It's true; he does spend time looking at trees. "There are certain kinds of wood I'm always looking for," like white cedar, burls of oak and cherry, and yellow birch. But he's not looking now; he's hardly looking out the window at all, and driving too fast to see much of anything. He instinctively slows down but feels he might have already made himself obvious and open to scrutiny.

There is not much else to see, just more of the same. After another stretch of driving, he turns the truck toward home. The light of day has faded by the time they reach the house. It is a more traditional time for dinner. After entering the house, he brings up the fire again, moves to the kitchen and checks the pot of stew. He sets the table with bowls and spoons and adds a loaf of good bread and butter and a couple of knives, then offers Corbin to help himself. After ladling stew into his bowl, he sits down to eat and seems to like it. After they are done eating, they watch television together until it becomes obvious Corbin is tired, and he encourages him to go to bed. Soon after he goes to bed himself.

The morning reveals snowfall as predicted. The forecast seems about accurate with accumulation of four or five inches. After making a cup of coffee, he stands before the glass sliding door staring out at a world of fresh whiteness, the limbs of trees topped with snow, the one side of trunks covered white, indicating which way the wind blew. The storm seems to have moved on, leaving patches of sunshine filtering through the snowy branches with glittering crystals of flakes drifting down. The fresh snow is a nice greeting for Corbin on his first full day. The question again is what to do with him? He is reminded of the challenge of having to consider someone, but is also reminded that it won't be long before Corbin will be in school and he back to work, and focusing on the two of them together won't be such an issue. But for now, he has to make decisions. He is also aware of his commitment to have a serious talk with Corbin. He wanted it to be first chance, and is determined to get every-thing out in the open, set the tone, be honest about what they are up against. The situation isn't something either of them wanted, but must make the best of. It is important that Corbin hear it from him: that having Corbin live with him is not by default, but something he decided upon and is deter-mined to make positive. He has gone through the conversation many times in his head. His interest is to make Corbin comfortable, give him confidence, assure him that he isn't a bother, and that the goal of their living together is to make this a good thing, but it will take both their efforts. His thought was to have the conversation as soon as possible to get it over with, but in the brightness of day, the timing doesn't seem so urgent; it could feel forced, a bit contrived. Mostly the feeling comes from not being sure where Corbin is at; what is going on with him.

He feels at a loss for more than the first time in the last day, with the rest of the day still ahead. What does come to mind is a result of being out in the woods the previous day, with an additional element made available by the new snow; it's something he likes to do, has done plenty before; it could be interesting for Corbin. With the coming of bad weather, animals will hunker down in thick cover and ride out a storm, then afterward be on their feet, anxious to catch up on their feeding. It is then they make new tracks easily visible, revealing the number of animals in an area and the patterns of travel, which direction they move, where they prefer to feed and bed. It is valuable information to a hunter, especially of deer, which is what he likes to do. When learning a new area, he will spend hours driving roads looking at tracks before committing to putting on boots to learn the area further. Hunting is a big part of his life, his avenue of involvement with nature, the way he feeds himself. He's not going to bring hunting to Corbin because it will be something important for him to come to terms with on his own; the idea of taking a life, the relationship with your food, one's place in the natural world.

With the next step with Corbin decided, he feels relieved.

The matter then is when Corbin will be up and out of his room; as a teenager, he might sleep until noon, especially with all the gyration he has been through in the last few days; it could have taken a lot out of him.

He decides to hold off on having breakfast to see if Corbin comes to join him. He could use the time to load some more wood from the garage, but decides to wait until later. It is something Corbin can help with; it can be one of his responsibilities; cutting and stacking and keeping supplied with wood is a big deal. Helping with wood can be a way for Corbin to contribute.

A text message comes to his phone. He is already hoping, when he sees it is from Lucy. If he hadn't heard from her soon, he would have contacted her. "How be uncle Floyd". He is sure she has been wondering about him and his initial time with Corbin. "Hangin in there". He is glad for the chance to connect. "All good" comes back to him. He takes a moment, wanting to be accurate, "Bit up in the air". He waits for a response. "K to stop over". He is pleased, "Sure".

A change of plans. But also, a sudden relief. He had intended to drive with Corbin to the woods as soon as they finished breakfast, but with Lucy coming over, that would have to wait. And her meeting Corbin sooner than expected will only be a good thing. Lucy will be great with Corbin, and it will take some pressure off him.

But after sending the text, he wonders if his response was telling enough. "Sure" could be open to interpretation; could mean anytime, in the next hour or the next day. And he really wants to see her. The possibility of that not happening accelerates the feeling of having a lot to tell her; she is important to him. He adds to his text, "Soon?" "Available" comes back to him. He responds, "Yes".

It still isn't enough. He wants to see her as soon as possible. The thought of waiting to see her suddenly grips him; Lucy has been with him through this whole process with Corbin, has been his confidant, his sounding board; he has leaned on her experience with her own two daughters. The feeling only grows until he texts her again, "ASAP?" She is the person he trusts, the person he is in love with, the person he is considering spending the rest of his life with.

Nothing comes back; she is either on her way or away from her phone; he'll have to wait. If she left right away, reaching him would take ten minutes. Any waiting beyond that will be difficult. And he is faced with another dilemma. The last thing he wants now is for Corbin to come out of his room; he really wants some time to himself with Lucy. As soon as she could arrive, he stays aware of the driveway out the window. After another few minutes, he considers texting her again.

But she does come. After exiting her vehicle, he doesn't wait for her to reach the front door before opening it. It is good to see her. At first glance, she is always more beautiful than he remembers. Their eyes meet and they exchange a quick kiss. Then without giving her a chance to take off her coat, he whispers her silent, and taking her arm, whisks her across the room toward the kitchen, concerned that if Corbin hears someone at the door, he might come out. She looked up with eyes surprised, his only assurance to smile back as he reached the kitchen and turned, before backing into the far corner of the counter and pulling her in. "Shhh," he reiterates, but her expression doesn't change. She looks up at him with eyes wide, from just below his chin, "What's going on?"

His reaction is to give a quick laugh, both admitting his folly and attempting to convince that everything is alright, when everything isn't alright, just not as bad as she might be thinking. Her focus narrows, staring into him. "Is Corbin alright?" It's the big question, what he is trying to decide, but his first interest is to appease her in general terms, "Yes, yes, yes." But he doesn't want to gloss over his concerns, "I mean, I think so," because he doesn't want to give her the wrong impression either, "I'm sure he's got ten fingers and toes." And she not buying any attempt at lightness; he needs some kind of explanation that gets to the heart of the matter. "I don't know," he says, lowering his head, communicating an honest dismay, "It's the craziest thing." And she just looking at him as if he hadn't said enough. "I just can't get a feel for this kid."

Still she doesn't say anything as if waiting for more, not demanding just waiting, not to be encouraging or to rescue him. "I think he might be depressed," he says, then not saying anything new but saying the same thing in a different way, like going sideways, "There might be something wrong with him." And she just looking but really trying to understand, "You said he's quiet."

Yes, he said quiet, but this is beyond quiet; it could be something essential, like something defective. "He's got a lot going on," she says, stating the obvious, and the obvious is the place to start of course, but he is trying to move beyond all that, because he is stuck with it and it's not going away. "It's only been a day." And yes, more of being obvious, as if the obvious is adding up to be something solid, like some kind of counterweight, so he feels forced to shift back to the other side to balance the scale. "There's just something off."

Her look is questioning, but she also laughs, not as counterpoint but being the voice of reason, and him willing to consider reason but not dismiss possibility, so he stays on the side tapped into his fear that keeps opening and hasn't reached the bottom. "He could be a lost soul." She laughs even further. It's what gets his attention as a new direction, something more positive that he wants to extend, but also needing to reach the end of from where he has been, a little further, like mixing them together. "What if he turns out to be some kind of delinquent?" And her incredulous enough to shake her head, putting hands to his chest and leaning back, but with arms around, he pulls her in, feeling the edges of her hips against him. "He could be a maniac."

Now she is definitely amused but having none of it. "You're an idiot," she says, taking a jab at him.

It's his turn to laugh; he's only pleased with himself, the change he has caused, the smile in her eyes, the spread of her mouth; he has reached the place of two of them. "Yeah, but I'm your idiot." And she tilts her head back, mouth open, a further laugh, not as dismissing, but admission enough herself, of everything they are, as something that expands, as some effervescence, some kind of mingling.

And he released to something greater because it's there, where he wants to be, the power of his own life in the wonder of a woman, in the confirmation of them, so that the words come easy with no reservation, as statement of everything they have talked about, a leap to fully embodied, "You know I'm going to marry you."

And she not denying, and with a different kind of admission, a punctuation of giving quick jabs of her hips while pushing at him and him holding her back, as evidence of her being affected, like ringing a bell. "Well, you better not pull any of that down-on-one-knee crap," she says as the kind of confirmation to where they have been, but the feeling of one step further, to a place that leaves no doubt, "It's gonna be an executive decision."

And him a kind of relief, in a spirit of revelation, in a wash of goodness, released to a direction, as all he ever wanted, in the promise of two people as good man and good woman, opening to full expression, maybe even deeper. "I'm gonna ask you again."

THE FUNNY WAY YOU
SAY HELLO

The first time was on a Sunday night. The place was dead, except for the few people sitting ringed around the bar on stools. Beneath the lights on stage across the darkened room, a lone guitar player sang to empty tables and chairs. I watched the woman seated—young but olding, with heavy make-up and heavy arms—because she was drunk and loud.

"Hey, hey," she half yelled, flapping her hand like a handkerchief at the end of her wrist. "Hey, Carlos."

Unable to avoid her any longer, the bartender finally walked over, and spreading his hands along the counter, directly met her gaze. "Yes?"

"I'd like another drink please," the woman stated sprightly, hiking herself up on her stool.

"You already have a drink," the bartender said, pushing her half-full glass to in front of her.

"Well can't I have two?

The bartender continued to match her gaze. "And after this, I think that's enough," he replied with obvious curtness.

The bartender turned away. The woman stared after him in mock indignation, before breaking into a high, taunting shrill. "Oh Carlos! Please Carlos! Just one more Carlos!"

It was then that the man seated next to the woman came rocking forward until almost against her. The woman turned surprised.

It is the first I can remember of the man. For as much as I have tried—he sat almost directly across the bar from me, and with only a few people in the place, I had to have noticed him—but nothing stuck with me. Somehow, the man completely escaped my scrutiny. Even after the woman pushed him away, he appeared completely unfocused. Mostly it was that face of his: the heavy eyelids, the blank wooden stare. Because of his sports coat, I guessed him to be somewhat professional, obviously middle-aged.

Somehow the man got the woman to dance. With him following behind, the woman led through the shadows to the empty floor and was already moving in elongated sweeps to the music when the man entered and started into short jerks of his arms and legs, imitating a rhythm. In the dim light and silhouetted against the darkened stage, the woman became a gypsy throwing back her head and raising her arms, weaving a spell of music and motion. Oblivious to the music, the man shuffled after her, the jerking of his arms and legs thinly veiling his advance.

Soon a game developed. The man approached the woman, methodically directing her toward a corner of the floor. She let him take her so far before escaping in a glide or sudden pirouette. The man simply turned to her new direction. In the middle of the floor, the woman danced to herself.

On one of her escapes, however, the man snatched an

end of the scarf the woman had been flaunting around her neck, and before she could check her momentum, the length of scarf extended out with the man, until it took a snatch of her own to grab the other end. The arena of their game had suddenly decreased greatly in size. The woman still danced with the same flitty abandon, but with the scarf, she now had the arm of a partner. Swinging under the scarf, she wrapped herself a turn in it then spun herself out and circled around.

Handful by handful, the length of scarf began to disappear through the man's hands. The woman continued to ignore him until almost in his arms. Only then did she confront the man. With both their hands at his chest holding the scarf, they stood face to face, motionless in the lights beyond the darkness. They could have been lovers. The poignancy of the moment became dramatic. Then the man's face shifted. Even from where I sat, I could see his face break wide into a leering grin. The woman's composure instantly shattered. Drawing back, she violently shoved the man, then left the dance floor. Without lifting her head, the woman got her coat and left the place.

What had I seen? As the man slowly made his way back to the bar, I waited for some further clue. Yet stepping out of the shadows and again taking his seat almost directly across from me, the man gave no indication whatsoever that anything remarkable had happened. His manner was completely indifferent; there was no effort to hide anything or act in any particular way. He stared ahead and casually returned to his drink.

Yet I couldn't deny what I had witnessed. The moment had been explosive—in an instant, the woman in all her puffery had been decimated. How did that happen? I was sure the man had proceeded with intent, determination; I felt in the delivery of his grin a deliberate sense of timing. Yet watching him from across the bar, I saw no sign of any such vitality. Believing he sensed me watching him, I kept my eyes averted, and only occasionally glanced to look. But I was always met by the same vacant stare. The man was stoic, sterile, as if his being had receded far into him. With his heavy eyes and round face, he had the laconic look of a lazy toad. The more I stayed aware of him, however, the more I sensed a depth to his vacancy. Beneath the facade, I imagined the man to be gloating in his conquest.

Seeing the man the second time, however, left little doubt as to what he was up to. Even on a Saturday night, with the place packed and a band playing, I recognized the herky-jerk of his shoulders amongst the dancers. I had caught him in the middle of an encounter. Dancing with a woman, he kept his distance until she opened to the music. Slowly he moved in under the cover of her abandonment. Not until he was against the woman did she turn her attention to the man. With his arms connected around her, she struggled politely, then more assuredly. Face to face they were suspended. The man's vacant gaze then broke wide into that wicked grin. The woman rushed from the floor.

My impressions were confirmed! The man knew exactly what he was doing! As I watched transfixed, his whole play unfolded.

The man obviously knew what he was after, which women would vehicle his performance. They were never the prettiest women, always at least slightly heavy, with a genial manner to compensate for their physical insecurity. He approached them when they were most alone, the swirl of activity spinning beyond them. With a slight bow of his head that suggested everything gallant in a man, he asked them to dance.

As they danced, the man was in constant attention to the woman. He let her dictate the dancing, depended on her, paid homage to her by trying to imitate her far more fluid movements. The woman grew comfortable, swooned in his attention, and let the music take her. Assured a second dance, and under the veil of her abandonment, the man started his advance. At first, it was only an inching forward, as if caused by the pressure of the surrounding crowd. A hand was included lightly at her waist. The woman accepted out of graciousness or compassion, and the man proceeded. The woman initially attributed his pressure to awkwardness or drunkenness, then tried to ignore it as just a phase. But his advance grew stronger until he connected his arms around her and pulled her in. The woman struggled politely, and then true panic rose. Finally, she was forced to confront what had connected to her and fully look at the man, only to have that vacant face she had so much trusted crash wide into that leering grin. Devastated, the woman rushed from the floor.

The man was a predator! It was like watching a feeding frenzy. And he got away with it! At any moment, I expected the woman's friends to gather and confront him or for the club's staff to be notified. But nothing happened. The man simply returned to his place along the wall, standing with the others watching the dancers, absently surveying the crowd.

Three times I watched the man perform his strange routine. It was difficult to keep track of him through the crowd, but standing from my seat at the bar, I made sure to keep him in sight. It was as if I had stumbled upon a strange wonder. The man was in total control. He manipulated the scene perfectly. And no one seemed to notice! He had found a niche!

Yet I had noticed. The fact captured my attention. Could I have been the only one? To me the man was glaring. How could he even think he could get away with something like that? How long had it been going on? I could feel a confidence coming from the man, even a smugness. The world had opened up and made a place for him. He found a direction and pursued it with vigor.

Later that night, when the man walked to where he kept his coat and prepared to leave, I put my coat on as well. I had nothing specific in mind; I just wasn't ready for the man to leave me. Outside the bar, the man was already walking to my left down the street, so I turned up my collar to the chilled night and followed him. The man wasn't far ahead, and against the upright length of buildings that stretched down the block, he walked relaxed and without hurry. He had had a good night. Everything had gone in his favor. Then at the corner, he paused to let a car pass. In a move that continued to impress me, I reached for a cigarette and, coming up beside the man, asked him for a light.

The man turned to me, then absently raised a lighter. My heart was beating. I had already gone farther than I could have imagined. Would the man recognize me from the first night, when we sat across the bar from each other? Did he even suspect I knew what he was up to? Bending forward, I peered through the flame into that face of laconic laxness. The man gazed fully toward me, yet his eyes remained flat and empty. I waited for some flicker of awareness to rise to the surface, but he remained whole and impenetrable. I held out as long as I could. My cigarette lit, I was forced to withdraw. The man turned and walked across the street.

Now the man is here! I knew he'd be here. Even when I thought of him not coming, I knew he'd come. And tonight it will be easy for him. With a good crowd on hand, there are plenty of women. When the band starts up, I sense him stir.

His first choice is delightful! I picked her out immediately—a red-haired woman fallen past thirty. When she is alone, the man approaches and, with a slight bow of his head, asks her to dance. Hardly looking at him, the woman readily accepts. Following her to the floor, the man breaks into his methodical herky-jerk.

It all proceeds so neatly. By the second dance, the woman is open to the music, and under the spell of her abandonment, the man makes his move. When she finds him too close, he is already attached to her.

Pow! Just like that. The man's face flashes wide to deliver his grin. Devastated, the woman rushes from the floor. Seated again amongst her friends, she is obviously fuming but doesn't say a thing, and the man returns to his place along the wall.

He gets away with it! How does that happen? There should be an uproar. The man should be pummeled within an inch of his life! But nothing happens. The man simply stares out amongst the dancers and people seated.

Because of the crowd, it is not easy to see him. Standing toward the back along the wall, all I can really see is his face. The man's vacantness is absolute. I try to anticipate his next move and sense the build-up. I have looked the women over closely and believe it is only a matter of which one is available.

She is a woman I picked out near the front. The man is good, and waits just a moment after the last of her friends at the table is asked to dance. Approaching the woman, he could be the devil himself, and she would be glad for the offer.

Still, it isn't easy to see, and I am forced to step forward to keep a clear glimpse of the man. Again, he proceeds in his direction. His attention to the woman is flattering. And all the while that face, that blessed face of his, as vacant and open as to be anything she wants him to be. Even from where I am, I can sense his control. By the second song, he has already moved in. The hand at her waist goes unnoticed; the crush of the crowd could easily cause his moving against her. When she feels his pressure, it is already too late.

The man is a scream—the way he holds the woman until her panic peaks, before delivering his grin! The woman rushes from the floor, and the man just stands there, awash in his thrill. It is a wonder he doesn't just fall down in delight. I'm the one left shaking my head. He might as well be sticking in a knife.

And he gets away with it! It's not that he's so smart. How can they not see him? The man should be hoisted on a pole. Does he even know how lucky he is? If it weren't for that crazy face of his, he would never get away with something like that.

As the man returns to his place along the wall, I try to stay watching him, but have to step forward just to keep him in view. Even then, it is hard to see through the crowd. And I want to see the man. I've figured him out. It's like watching some freak force of nature.

It is impossible to keep the man in view, however, people

have moved in front of him. With no other choice, I follow further with the crowd that shuffles around the perimeter. There is the feeling of walking and being amongst the people, but I keep my focus on the man, I want to stay watching him. What dominates me is that the man doesn't have a clue anyone is on to him. He has to know he lives dangerously.

What if I asked his women to dance before he does? I could sense him about to make his move and make it before him. At first, the man might think it coincidence, but if it happened again, then again, he'd realize someone was on to him. But could I make it happen? It is not easy asking women to dance. I surely don't have the man's experience, and I don't have his face.

For now, I only want to get close to the man. The flow of the crowd is slow. My concern is that he will ask a woman to dance before I get there, but his pattern is to take a while for a momentum to build. I try to relax and let the line of people move me.

Making my way down the side wall toward the stage will bring me straight to the man. My idea is to get close then step aside and stand watching him. As the line of people continues, I get a glimpse of the man up ahead. The challenge will be to not be noticed. I think of his face and how it works for him. As I get close, I begin retreating. Further and further, I recede into myself. I want all trace of awareness to disappear.

There are three people between the man and me. Then there are two. I focus on retreating. My face is a facade, a surface floating on an ocean.

The person in front of me passes and the man is before

me. I try to ease from the flow of the crowd but it isn't easy. People are close together. I feel forced to turn sideways toward the man and almost push against him as I step in. I am up against the man. He turns to see me then looks away.

Then suddenly he looks at me again. The man is looking at me. I feel a reaction rise but hold myself against it, and stare straight ahead matching the man's vacantness.

It takes all my effort. Then as he looks at me, there is something different; an interest or puzzlement; I feel his scrutiny. The man looks away, then looks at me again.

He is searching my face. I try to be oblivious but there is a pressure rising. I fight against giving any indication and stay staring straight ahead. But he is looking at me—something is registering!

His eyes are opening. I struggle against the pressure.

The pressure is in my chest then into my face. The man's eyes keep opening in recognition. He begins backing away.

I try but I just can't hold on any longer. Suddenly I explode in laughter. The laughter is so much that I bend over. When I look up, the man's eyes are thrown wide.

I got him! The man's façade has completely shattered! He pushes back against the crowd. It's just too funny!

Suddenly the man turns and rushes onto the floor amongst the dancers.

He is getting away! I don't want the man to get away. In a panic, I start after him.

Through a jumble of arms and bodies, the man pushes through the crowd. I try to keep up with him.

The crowd slows his progress. His eyes flash in terror as he looks over his shoulder.

The man makes it across the dance floor and starts up the

other side. Again, it is an effort to keep up as I push through the crowd. When he reaches the place where he has left his coat and grabs it, everything changes, however. The man is leaving. I have no intention of letting the man leave me. As we pass toward the door, I grab my coat from along the wall and hurry after him.

Outside the bar, the man has a head start but isn't far in front, and I turn left and run after him. He runs for all he is worth, his arms and legs churning, his coat flapping at his side. But for all his effort, he isn't going very fast. Soon it becomes obvious I am going to catch him. The man reaches the street corner and rushes through the intersection with me close behind.

The absurdity catches up with me. I am running down the street after the man! All I wanted was to get close to him, and now I am running down the street! I can feel my arms and legs pumping and my breath.

The man runs completely panicked. What does he think is going to happen? He's been expecting me. The realization causes me to laugh. Watching the flailing of his arms and legs causes me to laugh louder. The laughter puts a charge into the man but doesn't carry him far.

Soon the man begins to fade. There is the slightest swerve in him as he runs, and within the next few strides, he is actually staggering.

The man can't go on. He drops his coat.

Suddenly he collapses against a car and jerks on the door handles. What is he doing? When that doesn't work, he staggers to the next car and jerks on the handles again. I am shocked. The man is in absolute terror. When the doors don't open, he stumbles to the next car and jerks on the handles.

In exhaustion, he finally falls back against the car. It's really too much. The laughter comes spilling out of me.

Because of the shadows, his billowing breath and my own breath, I can't see the man's face. And I want to see his face—I want to see how he looks at me. When my breath is under control, I move closer to the man. His own breathing has subsided, but there are still shadows, so I move closer.

But as the face comes into focus, I am surprised—the eyes are open, the mouth is open, but he is only staring at me —there is still that vacantness.

The man is still playing his game.

I move closer to in front of him, waiting for his reaction. I want to see the moment when his face breaks open, when he fully recognizes me. But nothing changes. There is that same sense of him retreating into himself, that same vacantness.

There's no way he's going to get away with this. He's just a pathetic little man. Even his dumb face can't save him.

I wait a moment, and when nothing changes, I step directly in front of him and confront his gaze. But nothing changes. He acts like he can't even see me.

Does he think I'm stupid? To get a reaction, I push at him, but he stays staring straight ahead. Again, I push him.

Suddenly the man begins to slide down the car. What is happening? He is starting to collapse. In a rush, I move forward and hoist him up by his collar.

Face to face, I stare at the man, boring my gaze into his eyes.

Yet his gaze remains absolutely empty.

Does he really think he can get away with this?

I shake him once, but nothing.

This has gone on long enough, and again I shake him.

His body feels slack. I realize if he is doing this on purpose, he could just as easily continue, and I push him against the car, but nothing. I push him again. Nothing.

Stepping back, I watch as the man's body hangs backward against the car. There is a subtle shift, then slowly sinking, the man's body gathers momentum until in a sudden rush he collapses in a heap at my feet.

The man is lying at my feet! I can't believe it! Looking around at the deserted street, the absurdity continues to expand—I am standing over the man on a deserted street in the empty night.

But there's no way he's going to get away with this. When nothing happens, I kick him. The game is over, so again I kick him.

This has gone on long enough. The man just lies there, so I kick him. When nothing happens, I kick him again. The rotten bastard, and again I kick him.

THE BACKWARD HOUSE

O n the road leading south from the village, that winds closer to then further away from the coast, sits a house sticking out from the edge of a thick line of forest extending in both directions across a vacant field of forty or so acres, grown over with tall weeds and interspersed with a few small cedar bushes. The house is a simple "A" frame of weathered wood, once painted but never since, that harkens back to a time of courageous and desperate people intent on carving back the forest in an attempt at farming. The results are obvious as an effort long ago abandoned, and the house, field and forest, stand in proximity and juxtaposition, depicting in portrait some landscape tableau of a bygone past. The only indication of any attempt at upkeep or modernization is the two upright and arched windows inserted into what had once been the blank face at the rear of the house. But all effort stopped there, begging the question as to why someone would put in just the two windows, which by themselves seemed out of place surrounded by empty space, and not add a door, which had an obvious and ideal location in the middle of the face, and wouldn't have cost much, and made perfect sense as additional access to avoid having to walk around the house to gain entrance.

For the originators of the house, the omission of even windows might have been purely one of limited resource, and if only one door was to be located in the house, it best be placed on the other side, where a door opened to probably a yard of farm implements and maybe a shed of tools or barn of animals. After the homestead became established, the refrain from adding a second door might have been a matter of strategy or instinct to avoid the tendency toward scrutiny and fixation to constantly monitor the incremental and too-meager growth of crops in a too-cool climate or feel forced to scrutinize and measure the persistent damage and decimation of anything planted, by the horde of animals marauding out from the surrounding forest at night to eat anything in sight. But what about the more recent owners? What was their excuse? Besides the seeming short-sightedness of saving on the cost of adding a second door and missing out on the benefit of gaining easier access, the even greater offense seemed to be against the very hierarchy of human needs. Because the house was blessed with a marvelous view; the kind of view people would covet and kill for, not only the area residents who treasured their connection and unobstructed proximity to nature as the measure and corner-stone of a rich and meaningful life but also the people from downstate and beyond, who would pay big money and roamed the countryside near and far searching for that most perfect view as a slice of heaven, to not only fulfill their highest hopes and dreams of what it meant to be fully alive embraced in the power and purity of mother nature, but to be fully released from all their past failures and sins including maybe even the original.

The house had it all. It offered the epitome of pastoral breadth and serenity. Without another house in sight, it sat perched atop a gentle slope, looking out over a golden expanse of field sweeping down to rolling hills of endless trees and beyond to the water of the great lake, barely seen but fully experienced in the cooling breezes that drifted out and over in the heat of summer. Facing a westerly direction, the house was blessed with a string of endless sunsets. How could someone not take advantage of such an opportunity? After the two windows were installed, people waited for some further renovation as the natural course of things, but nothing happened. As it was, the house seemed unfinished and, more than that felt condemned to be facing the wrong direction. The essence of human civility was that a house should look out at the world and face its neighbors. To continue to face the other way seemed unnatural, deliberate, an affront to sensibility, a full-fledged rejection and conscious assault to decency, a blatant disregard, purposeful, an expression of personal pathology. Eventually, it got to the point of people staring at the two arched windows that a feeling developed of the windows staring back, with the look of two raised eyes, that eventually took on the look to folk of a beloved cartoon character from years past, and the house came to be called "The Felix-The-Cat House", but enough people weren't familiar with the character, so the house simply became known as "The Backward House."

For as long as most people could remember, the house was owned and occupied by Carl and Liz Pruitt. Liz had summered in the area with family as a child, through being a young adult at a cottage rented from one of the local resorts. Carl and Liz vacationed at times in the area with their own family, then after Liz took early retirement from her position as a health administrator, they bought the old farmhouse and moved in permanently. Carl started a small survey business, which was his trade, never employing more than another person or two, and developed a reputation for being honest and dependable. Carl was stout of medium height, with thick mustache and matching dark hair that belied his years advancing past middle age. If there ever was a complaint about him, it was that he moved too fast and could get ahead of himself, which caused him to be abrupt with people. Liz helped keep the books of her husband's business and, at times hired herself out to other area businesses to do the same kind of work. Liz was thin with thin shoulders, making her seem taller, and pleasant looking with poised brown eyes behind oversized glasses that highlighted her longish face, framed by wavy brunette hair. As a couple, they could be seen on occasion sharing a meal at a local eatery, though rarely in the company of others. It was thought Liz had closer friends out of town because of time spent away.

Most of her socializing locally was connected to her volunteer work. Liz focused on helping organize some of the larger area events, mostly in summer and usually associated with the different art fairs and music festivals that sprung up like flowers to cater to and attract the many hundreds, even thousands of people, who flooded to what one national media outlet designated "The most beautiful place in America." Liz never took the lead in any such endeavor but was one of the trusted and dependable foot soldiers on whom the success of any such event depends. Her just reward as the fruits of her labor seemed to be that when the event did take place, she could be seen walking amongst the crowd arm-in-arm with Carl, basking in good cheer, visiting and talking with friends and people they knew. Liz was bright and energetic. It was understood that Carl would likely never attend such events on his own, but in the company of his wife, he could be engaging and affable.

And it was through connection to volunteer work that most people came in contact with her amazing home. Liz was never quick to invite company, though she didn't shy from it either, and most of her offers were in reciprocation for having been invited somewhere herself, usually under the guise of advancing the work on some shared project. But a visit to her house was seen as something special, something looked forward to, even as an added feature of something possible, as something motivating to join Liz's efforts. Because people previously visiting talked about the experience of her house in such glowing terms, often with the fanfare of being witness to a marvel, with the effect of no two people describing the experience quite the same, the future initiate felt forced to find out for themselves and preparing for the moment felt a bit anxious but with heightened anticipation, so that almost uninformedly the attempt was made to adopt an attitude and approach of sustained nonchalance, in an effort to thus balance against the amazement they expected to encounter and the desire to maintain a fine sense of decency and decorum.

Arriving at the house, a person would be greeted at the side entrance by Liz, typically dressed in something long and flowing. The first thing noticed upon entering was the flood of natural light emanating from the two arched windows at the one end and extending to every corner, reflected in the soft dove-grey color of the walls continuing to the full height of the modestly vaulted ceiling of the great room, giving the internal size of the home a much bigger feel than expected, and a great surprise, most because the effect was never mentioned in any description by anyone having visited. Toward the other end of the house and under a low ceiling, a long table extended toward a smallish kitchen. Beyond a full bank of windows stretched across the far end of the house, giving full view to a length of porch extending beneath an overhang. This was where the real event began, the direction where all manner and sense of magnitude and expectation were directed. Stepping out through the door and along the porch, a person was met by a dense and complicated land-scape of rising trunks and great twisting limbs beneath a thick canopy of leaves blinking dappled sunlight, causing some to profess half expecting trolls to pop up from the enchanted understory or forest fairies to flitter about amongst the trees.

But that was just the start. With the casual air of a tour guide, Liz led from the porch down a couple of steps onto a flat-stone walkway that extended further to what at first appeared as a wall of evergreen and deciduous bushes that separated into alcoves connected yet secluded as some kind of maze, a veritable Art Park. Each display of sculpture was individual and distinguished, as the distinct space of some great magnificence of carved and curved and polished wood, or shiny metal twisting and extending into great configura-tions and expressions of fantastic shapes, or expansive conglomerates of colored and clear glass cut and jangled to capture and refract diffused light. One station led to another.

There were more than a dozen, each item of magnificence a world to itself, transcending into such a strong statement of vision and imagination, sparking some confirmation of wonder and magnitude for what was even possible.

The cumulative effect escalated to ooohs and aaahs that escaped any previous intention to be restrained and invariably led to wondering if Liz indeed was at least one of the artists herself, and she, with a flick of the wrist and toss of the hand and subsequent surprise of laughter, as if the mere thought was the most absurd thing imaginable, dismissed the inquiry completely. Yet she was undoubtedly at the center of everything collected and created as the gathering force, the curator if nothing else, in a display of pure artist sensibility, as expression of depth and power of affect, a bona fide genius in her own right. The sculpture park placed her in highest esteem amongst those initiated, ensuring her a status of respect and gratitude, in appreciation for bestowing a great gift, if nothing else, the feeling of being made to feel special. So a visit to the house created a bond of privilege, the foundational aspect of a shared secret, the feeling of having entered a kind of club that ultimately had the effect of dividing people into those who had visited and those who hadn't.

"It's like she's giving us the finger," says Creed Thompson, as one who hadn't been invited to the house, would never be invited, and wouldn't accept even if he were invited, in response to hearing her name mentioned, just as he approached the three women seated at the restaurant table with coffee cups in hand, so that the utterance of the name

Liz Pruitt was perfect timing, as no accident, as something taken as testimony to how the world works, as full confirmation of his connection to the powers that be, as his reward for not only being open and available but also in good standing. Not that he wouldn't have sat amongst the women anyway, that being determined as soon as he saw the empty chair as the kind of opportunity always looked for, but receiving the name Liz Pruitt as the perfect segway to deliver his entrance with the kind of wit and aplomb more accustomed to his standing and talent, understanding that his comment would have meaning to at least the one woman seated directly across the table he recognized if only vaguely, as assurance to her being well aware of Liz Pruitt in reference to her house and its controversy pervading and persistent if not to just below the surface, then a full-blown and prominent weave in the fabric of the area. And his utterance having the desired effect, maybe more than expected, as confirmation from the other two women he didn't know, as a nice surprise, like striking a chord or plucking a string, the eruption of spontaneous chuckle or laugh or something of that sort but reaction of recognition all the same, so that after letting his comment gather weight then be delivered as centerpiece to the table he followed and took his seat as his rightful place in the nature of things.

Creed Thompson was the local curmudgeon and gadfly who earned the bulk of his reputation by standing at local council and committee meetings at the time designated for public input and espousing some outlandish theory of conspiracy and cahoots usually associated with some issue of proposed progress, directed at the governing body in general or some leading member, alleging their support as the result of some perceived personal interest likely linked to ill-gotten financial gain. Creed Thompson could be sixty or eighty, with longish white hair, a matching beard, and beady eyes reaching out through wire-rimmed glasses. He had a wizened face of sallow skin and the demeanor of a cantankerous knot of muscle.

Across the table from him sits Kate Crowley, local business owner of the women's clothing boutique located on Main Street just down the block, solidly successful and solidly middle-aged, with a rounded face and well-coiffed roundish hair and tasteful make-up and modeling the latest fashion from her store, currently wearing a large-checked black-and-white plaid cape over sage-colored turtleneck perfect for the unseasonably cool fall weather presently being experienced.

And she has plenty of experience with Creed Thompson, not so much from the kind of meetings she rarely attended and he addressed, and she heard about, but from his wandering through town on a nearly daily basis, as the other key component of his public endeavor and subsequent persona, with him stopping in stores and establishments to ingratiate himself as a dominating force, which she was all but impervious to as the owner of a store exclusively selling women's clothes and accessories that he wouldn't be caught dead in no matter how much his need to bend an ear, causing her to be eternally grateful as an added benefit of her choice of endeavor, but aware of the many stories relaying his antics or tales of pontification and holding court and the different efforts and strategies of deflecting and defending and otherwise limiting or holding off or avoiding him altogether.

Now it is her turn to be subject to his personhood. As

soon as he walked through the door and his eyes noticing the empty chair the exact moment she registered the open seat herself from his point of view, knowing for a fact the three of them were in for it, but couldn't be avoided except in the attempt of making them available to some kind of miracle, she continued the line of conversation as if words themselves the power to deter his momentum or act as some kind of barrier which would be the course for any average person, but not Creed Thompson, with no regard for decorum or even decency, and she mentioning the name Liz Pruitt in the continuity of people being suggested to approach who might be willing to help in organizing their marketing committee for the upcoming Christmas festival. And he grabbing her name from thin air like grabbing a baton and twirling it for showing off as ingratiating fanfare, not that she was any great fan of Liz Pruitt and thus no great defender, but as one who had been to her house and didn't believe it to be the be-and-end-all but impressive enough that she would look forward to being invited again, and in the scheme of things if the world was divided into those she respected and those she didn't and such a ledger did exist, there being little doubt which opposite column the two of them fell, so that she wasn't about to tolerate Liz Pruitt or anyone else in her regard being besmirched by the likes of Creed Thompson, even if it might be construed there was hint of truth to his comment, but juxtaposed against the feeling that she was responsible for providing the name to instigate his avenue of entry to their group in the first place, as the leader who called the meeting, and the one who subsequently felt the duty to take the bull by the horns in handling the situation. "Well, you've never been shy in giving your opinion."

And Creed Thompson, taking the full brunt of her directive, not so much the force of it but the taste of it that could be hard to tell exactly like acerbic or ferment, looking at her in full scrutiny as if he were studying the man in the moon, taking full measure to determine his relationship, aware that he being met directly was no surprise, as how things often proceeded, the less-than-welcoming not lost on him, as even familiar, as often was the case. And him prepared, as in the nature of practice, to the point of refinement, in full confidence that the only thing needed was the chance to warm up to him if "warm-up" could ever be the proper term, but any development could hardly be expected all at once, and in that sense, time was on his side, like trusting gravity as an essential component of the universe itself. To emphasize his point as part of his charm, as culmination of acquired skill, in further attempt to ingratiate himself, not so much seeking permission but to further instill his presence, he took a moment as announcement and punctuation to run his hand straight back through his longish white hair then trace down his matching beard with thumb and index finger along the edges of his mouth stained yellow from tobacco, the gesture not unlike a lizard flicking its tongue as measure of scent and temperature before gallantly offering into the middle of them as their just reward. "I trust you ladies are enjoying yourselves."

And Kate Crowley Looking across the table at what has shown up in front of them, her only interest to continue her strategy of constructing a barrier, to meet head-on, not what she could stop but to hold the line against what could happen because it could be bad, in an attempt to fortify, as if she were driving in ground stakes, in the same manner as swinging a hammer. "We are having a meeting. I don't suppose you'd be interested in joining the Christmas festival's marketing committee?"

An immediate snigger emitting from the woman seated next to her, a younger but not youngish version of Kate Crowley herself, similar in overall size and shape but of lesser distinction, as if she were not yet fully aware of a similar path available to her life and not yet started. Patty Barlow wore a mauve-colored sweater and had full and falling dark hair, ample swipes of eyeliner, and maroon lipstick. She had a pleasant face of no great merit but big brown eyes that were undoubtedly her most distinguishing characteristic. The snigger she emitted was involuntary and the exact duplicate of her previous outburst released at the very start of the encounter when Creed Thompson delivered his initial indictment of Liz Pruitt in reference to her house, that caught her as the same kind of cutting-edge funny just struck in her again by the retort of Kate Crowley, but of such different source and reason, because her unconscious response to Creed Thompson had left her mortified at the possible interpretation that she not only acknowledged some truth to what he had stated but was agreeing with him, with the full weight of understanding that her spontaneous outburst put her at risk of not only being opposite with the women she was seated with, but on the other side of Liz Pruitt herself, as someone she had only met in the most casual of circumstance, but knew of connected to her magnificent house that caused Patty Barlow to harbor a wish to be invited someday herself, which was part of the latent and not clearly formed reason for her volunteering on different committees in the first place, as the extension of her working for an area nonprofit and making volunteering the cornerstone of her strategy to becoming a good person, but also to being ingratiated as one of the locals in the place she chose to live her life as part of the community. So the snigger in response to Kate Crowley's statement caused nothing less than relief as the chance to redeem herself in genuine and spontaneous fashion, leave little doubt as to which side of any exchange she was on, and show her acknowledgment and offer support as not only giving full permission to continue in what she perceived as a clear jab at Creed Thompson, but agreement of what should be done and what she would like to do if she were the one doing it.

To the other side and across the table sits Carly Lewis, the newcomer to the group and to the area, youngish of moderate size and modest stature, with pulled-back hair and a taste for clothes no one yet has experienced, and was surely not present in her current attire of solid forest-green chamois flannel shirt over scoop-necked black tee over classic jeans, that was a reflection of a strategy she has chosen to remain neutral in all matters of involvement with the area, as to avoid the chance to reflect back on herself, with the understanding that in matters especially of opinions there were always two sides to every story, and to give credence to any one side caused a shift toward complicity and agreement that caused by its nature a degree of commitment, and made it harder even downright impossible ever to backtrack and recover to any sense of neutrality, so best effort be made to take every reason and measure to avoid even a whiff of taking sides in the first place. Yet the one person who blew that strategy out of the water had come walking through the door in the person of Creed Thompson, igniting a pile of reaction to the man himself seen striding toward them and that empty chair, as the man she most heard about as the subject told of the most remarkable and outrageous tales, as maybe first and foremost causing her to be appalled he got away with such things, and wasn't decried and admonished and outright thrown out on his ear, as indication not in any way a contradiction to her commitment of staying neutral, but as just fact concluded from some hardearned understanding of the weakness of people in confronting both cruelty and injustice, personified in the person coming toward her as the conglomerate of all such men ever known or even heard about who bullied and badgered and forced their way through the world leaving good hearts and spirits in their wake to struggle and gasp, without even the slightest caring or concern or even awareness. Creed Thompson was a despicable human being of no redeeming value. The crust had formed around him. His very presence violated her every will and determination as something she was forced to endure and live with. And then for him to mention the name Liz Pruitt, the only other person, though not even remote in stature and intensity, who caused consternation and challenge to her strategy of not taking sides, after having been made very aware of both ends of the issue of Liz Pruitt and her house to the point of feeling pressured by pure force and volume in such strong and decided terms to take position, then forced to confront the situation further on almost a daily basis that had become her dilemma of having to drive back and forth past the house on her way to and from work as counter clerk in a neighboring town, to the point she actually took an alternative route more days than not to avoid the issue, even if it extended her drive by a whole eight minutes. So the situation of Liz Pruitt in conjunction and conjecture with Creed Thompson as two sides of a coin added together bearing both weight and pressure to become really too much and overwhelming, causing such a revolt to back up in her as the collapse of her intended life's volition like a house of cards, that she felt desperate enough and determined enough to avoid at all cost even the very air he breathed, as a reflex of preservation beyond mere protest, to the point of holding her own breath to the point of causing strain to the verge of actual discomfort.

Creed Thompson looks at one woman and then the other. To one side, a woman seems to be convulsing with bugged-out eyes and puffed-up cheeks, and to the other, a woman seems to be sputtering and stammering into her hands as she covers her face. And across from him, a woman glares as if she wants to eat him alive. The world is full of weirdos! Creed Thompson decides the situation is not something he couldn't win, but something he doesn't want to. To affirm his assessment, he takes a moment to run his hand back through his hair, then down his beard with thumb and forefinger along both sides of his mouth stained yellow with tobacco, stands straight up from his chair, and says before walking directly past the table. "Well, you ladies enjoy your meeting."

And so it goes in the life of the village, through the great changes of hot summer and deep snow, in the vague but persistent feeling that something is always coming and something else fading away. And the issue of The Backward House eventually did decide itself. Carl Pruitt was taken too soon by one of the cancers, and Liz continued on in declining health until two of her daughters moved her to assisted living. The house was put up for sale and sold. It was the dead of winter and no one moved in, indicating the house probably wouldn't be a permanent residence. Occasionally people could be seen coming and going, mostly on weekends. And without ever knowing, the new owners became the subject of great scrutiny and debate as to the outcome of the place. Eventually in the spring, building material was delivered and workers began showing up, and soon after a door appeared in the face of the house, equally distant between the two arched cat-eye windows. By summer a grand deck stretched across the exterior length. Groups of people could be seen enjoying barbeque and playing games in the large square of lawn cut out from the vacant field. Toward evening, people lounged in comfortable chairs, sipping drinks and basking in the glow of endless sunsets.

THE WILDERNESS EXPERIENCE

J ohn Henry Sands was just two years old when his father
was killed in the war in Vietnam. Yes, this was a
tragedy, though how much of an effect it had on him
was hard to say; he remembered nothing of the incident, and
at such a young age surely must have been protected from
the knowledge by those around him. Of course, the awareness still reached him. His first real memories of his father's
death being mentioned were in encounters with neighborhood kids, yet his impression was of having already been
well aware of the fact.

From there, the effect of his father's dying might best be
summed up by how it caused others to react to him. Growing
up, his father being killed was his most distinguishing characteristic, the thing people remembered about him long after
having known him. It even had its advantages. More than
once, his father having died was used to explain away John's
actions, and later when his first real girlfriend took off her
dress and brought him into her arms, he was sure it was a lot
of the reason.

Otherwise, John Henry had what could be considered a fairly normal childhood. He grew up near the center of town, had a sister, played basketball and baseball. The world happened as much around him as it happened to him. It was this feeling that urged John. He loved to feel the bigness of the world, with his arms spread and the wind blowing. Yet behind the majesty of the world lurked a darkness so dense and massive that it could blot out the sun. Because everything must die someday. It seemed so strange to just die and be gone. John Henry couldn't fathom death. Death was something he couldn't get his arms around.

No, the teen years weren't easy for John, though they hardly are for anyone, and maybe the best thing going for him was that he knew nothing else. It was just his life, and he still felt he was doing all right. In fact, if someone were to ask, he probably would say he was doing as well as anyone, maybe even better than most, but definitely with a way to go. John Henry liked life; he had a lot of life ahead of him; he was going to make the best of it.

It was during this time that his feelings about his father began to change. Until then, his father had continued to be not much of a factor. After all, he had never known his father, and there were plenty of kids who didn't get along with theirs.

But while in high school there were times when the thought came to him that his father had lived a life and had done things similar to what he was doing. The realization centered mostly on special events, like earning a varsity letter, his first big dance, and entering his senior year.

The occurrences continued through graduation then being out of school, until later that summer while up on a hill late one night, feeling his whole life expand and mingle freely with the lights of the city that spread beneath him, the feeling that his father had felt like this on a night like this was so strong, that John absolutely felt the presence of his father, not as a ghost or anything, but as an awareness bridging across time. What had his father really been like? Questions flooded him. If he and his father had known each other, they might have been friends.

Even his feelings about his father's enlistment in the army changed. John Henry could never imagine doing something like that and had always believed his father, having enlisted, distinguished the two of them. But it was a different time then, things were so unsettled. With so little of his own life settled, John wasn't so quick to decide on how things should be.

From that perspective, John liked feeling his father's presence. It gave him something to bounce his thoughts off. All he had to do was think about what his father might have thought or done in any situation, and he would get an impression.

However, his feelings about his father's presence changed when he learned the date his father entered the service. The notice was amongst some mementos his mother kept in a box. His father had entered the army just a few weeks before his nineteenth birthday. John would soon be turning nineteen. What would it be like going into the army and then going off to war? And his father wouldn't be coming back. When his father was his age, his father had less than a year to live. By then, John Henry had the feeling his father's life and his were traveling somewhat of a parallel path. Almost everything he was aware of saying and doing was now reflected against what his father might have said and done. Then to have it just end—where would that leave him? When John tried to answer the question, it felt strange to have nothing clear come to mind.

His initial reaction was to stop bouncing his thoughts off the presence of his father, but he found it wasn't so easy. Next, he concentrated on convincing himself that this whole thing with his father was just the imaginings of his mind. He could believe that, but it didn't seem to cause a change. An uneasiness began to grow. He had to admit it was starting to worry him. He wished he had someone to whom he could truly confide.

A solution did come to him, however. If he could somehow just be sure his father and he were not so much alike, then he could be fully convinced this connection with his father was just a fabrication. True, the little he knew about his father had come from photographs and a few impressions he got from other people, so no wonder his mind could create anything it wanted. Of course, he also ran the risk of finding he and his father really were alike, but if it came to that, he would just have to deal with it.

The obvious place to start deciding about his father was by asking his mother, and he should have been able to get everything he needed from her, but her recollections of his father had always been so obviously idealized that he felt he couldn't give her impressions any real credence. Both his father's parents were dead. There was a sister and a brother, but they didn't live in the area and weren't close to either John or his mother. He could ask some of his mother's relatives, but it would be an effort to approach them, and he would be open to having to answer questions himself.

Instead, he decided to pursue an idea he thought might really offer something. In the box of his mother's mementos there was a letter from a soldier who had served with his father, written a couple weeks after his father was killed, offering condolences for the tragedy and saying what a fine soldier his father had been, and what an honor it was to have served with him. The letter was actually quite formal, though the fact that it had been written at all intrigued John. But the way the letter ended caught his attention: "I will always remember him"—those last few words, thrown in at the end. They seemed a last-ditch effort to express what the soldier truly felt. John Henry imagined the soldier and his father might have been good friends, and the soldier would have known his father only as a young man. If he could locate the soldier, he could clearly understand what his father had been like. It felt like a bit of a crazy thing to do, but he was determined. First, he needed to know if the man had survived the war. After locating a list of those who had died and not finding his name, the next step was to contact the State Department for his address. John worked hard at making the letter specific and formal. As it turned out, it didn't matter, and a couple of weeks after sending the letter, he received a brief paragraph stating that kind of information wasn't released to the public. Disappointed but not deterred, he contacted local Veterans' groups to see if they could help. They didn't have any information but were glad to refer him to some national organizations.

However, at that time, an event occurred that changed everything. Years later, when looking back, the incident would be one of those events that divided his life into before and after.

Early one spring morning, while driving to his job as a helper laying carpet in one of those giant new homes, built in subdivisions springing up in what had recently been open country, the car in front of him hit a deer and came skidding to a halt. John slammed on the brakes to avoid becoming involved, which left him stopped behind the car and almost even with the deer that struggled on the other side of a small ditch. Immediately a woman came out of the car in front and rushed toward him as he got out of his car. "What should we do? What should we do?" she cried in panic as the deer struggled desperately. When he didn't have an answer, the woman rushed back to her car, saying she was going to a house to call the police.

The woman drove away, leaving John by himself with the deer. It was hideous. With at least two of its legs broken, the deer wasn't going anywhere, yet each time it exhausted itself trying, its inability to move caused it to panic, and the deer surged into struggling again. Would the police come? How long would it take? The deer's agony built in John until he was nearly running around. When an idea did come to him, he went directly to the trunk of his car and got out a utility knife he carried for work. He wondered if he could do what he had in mind. But the deer was suffering horribly. John Henry had always considered himself capable of doing what needed to be done. Now was the time to prove it.

With the deer's struggle becoming more intermittent, John approached it with slow, cautious steps and a constant soothing tone. The deer's initial reaction was to surge into panic again, but finally it just watched him, either calmed or too exhausted to move. Reaching the deer, John eased down and began lightly stroking its neck. Surprisingly the deer let him, and he concentrated on being as soothing as possible. What amazed him was the size of the deer: it was as big as a person, with a full, heaving chest.

John forced himself to focus on what needed to be done. Continuing to stroke the deer's neck, he felt the large pulsing vein and gently parted the hair. Switching the knife to his other hand, he touched the blade to the skin. Hesitating a moment to gather himself, he made a quick drawing motion with his arm.

The deer flinched and there was a quick spurt of blood, but John forced himself to be calm, and the deer settled back down. As the blood flowed, he continued to pet the deer. Lifting his head, John noticed they were on the edge of a field that swept out into a land of fields and farms, stretches of woods. Only then was there a serious threat of tears. This was the deer's land, the fields it roamed, where it had lived its life.

Still the deer didn't die. John couldn't believe how much blood was in it. A large puddle had formed on the ground, forcing him to let his boots get wet rather than move away. By this time the woman had returned and remained sitting in her car parked on the side of the road. John braced himself against what others might think, determined to see things through to the end.

The end did come, though another surge by the deer caused John to spend the last moments standing a few feet away. There were the twitching spasms, the last heaving of breath, and a full settling into quietness. When it was over, he returned to the roadside just as the police pulled up. They seemed surprised at what he had done but didn't say much.

He was asked to give a statement for the woman's accident report, and then finished his drive to work.

Nothing like that had ever happened to John before. For days the experience rose up around him. Reflecting back on it, new impressions and details came, and when he told the story to people he knew, he stayed very aware of his reactions.

The encounter with the deer also mixed with the issue of his father—death and dying. At times, the two experiences stood a distance apart and offered perspective and meaning to each other, while at other times, they combined to become a potent volume that seemed to lift him in a swirl.

The result was that the day marking his age as the same as when his father died came upon him quicker than expected. What was even more surprising was that he could look back and see his fixation with the idea of his father. In that sense, he was pleased that his encounter with the deer had at least broken his obsession.

Yet John Henry decided to stick with his original plan of commemorating the day of his father's death by spending it up north in the woods. The idea had stemmed from the notion that there might be some kind of anguish he would have to pass through—at one time, he actually imagined he might die himself, or somehow just disappear—and he didn't want anyone else around. But there was also the feeling of just wanting to be alone. The woods was always the place where he felt most comfortable. In his youth, he had spent time each summer with a friend up at a family cottage, and there was a lot of state land in the area, so he knew he could find a place to camp. As the day neared, he purchased a tent.

Along with his sleeping bag, John packed an ax and a

cooler. The drive would be several hours, and he wanted to take his time, so on the Friday morning, he was up early and on the road by ten o'clock. It was a nice day, and with the city fading behind and the open highway ahead, there was a feeling of anticipation and excitement. It had been too long since he had been up north. As the scenes of cities and people began to diminish, there was a feeling of land and trees.

The drive didn't seem as long as he remembered. Finally, leaving the highway, he stopped at a station for gas and a few last supplies. Driving on, he reached the forest and continued along the main road. The forest was big. It stretched for miles. With nothing else to do, he turned onto a narrow road and immediately became immersed in greenery.

For the time, John Henry was content to drive the dirt roads. The flickering of light and shadow amongst the brilliant green magnified a sense of density and space. As he became more concerned about not getting turned around, however, he started looking for a place to camp. He hoped to find a special site, preferably near water, maybe by a small lake or stream. But the only real water he found was a river lined with private property. A secluded place was still the priority, and finally he settled on a thick forest area that had tall trees. Turning down a thin side trail, he found a small opening that had likely been used as a campsite before.

After clearing leaves and brush from the site, he unloaded the car and set up the tent. Then it was a matter of finding wood. John Henry wanted a lot of wood. The night would be long and he wanted a fire. But most of the wood he found was fallen limbs, and dragging them back to camp was difficult because of the underbrush. Still he kept at it until most of the small opening around the tent was cluttered with dead branches. A saw would have been better than the ax, and after breaking up a good bunch of the branches with his feet, he used a flat stick to dig a fire pit.

He had planned on taking a walk, but after finishing the initial setup of camp, he decided to relax. Sitting on his cooler, sipping a beer, the peace and silence of the woods spread around him; it really was a superb evening. He became aware of the small sounds of animals and birds. However, the growing presence of mosquitoes soon forced him to light the fire. Some of the wood was wet and smoked horribly. He continually had to move to keep the smoke out of his eyes, but at least the bugs had lessened.

As evening continued to settle, John made final preparations to his campsite, then broke up more branches. With nothing else to do, he returned to sitting on the cooler. The thickening of the shadows added to the density and volume of the woods, but the light of the fire kept him comfortable. Being alone had never been much of a problem for John Henry, and it wasn't still, though as the darkness continued, there was a growing awareness of both himself and the space around him.

It was then that he decided to think about his father. It was what he was there for—the thought of his father had been hovering around him all day. With nothing else to do, he simply gave into it. When his father was his age, this was his last day on earth. What first came to him was an expanding reverberation of death. In contrast to his own almost glowing aliveness, the reverberation caused a sudden jolt. John Henry spent the next few moments centering himself.

Adding more wood to the fire, he focused on what needed to be done. This had gone on long enough. For almost two years, his father's presence had dominated him. With that in mind, he slowly opened himself; it was mostly a feeling of making himself available, and what came were more details and impressions of what had gone on with him and the idea of his father. But he had been through all that, and finding nothing new, he opened himself further. When his father was his age, this was his father's last day on earth. Again there was a dull reverberation. John at least knew he was moving in the right direction.

He thought of his father at war—the mixture of fear and bullets. What must it be like being surrounded by death, knowing it could just as easily be you?

John Henry had never traced his father's life to the end before. What was even more amazing was that he didn't even know how his father was killed; all his mother said was that the casket was closed, and she didn't care to find out. And it could be the key! If he knew how his father had died, he could take things through to the end. It was the only thing left for him.

He felt strong enough, and when the way felt open enough, he pushed ahead—his father in the army on the front lines. Staring into the fire, John envisioned the war vividly. The battle was definitely at night. The battle raged.

When the moment came, it was but a quick leap to imagine having a bullet in his heart with just a few seconds to live or having his legs blown off with just enough time to roll over and stare up into a star-filled sky. It was a star-filled sky, and he was staring up. There was a feeling of awe and terror. The verge of death. The death of his father.

John's heart pounded; he could feel his breathing escalate.

But as much as the intensity churned his insides, it didn't cause him to scream or yell, and he focused back in it.

The end: bombs and blood, gashed and mangled.

John Henry was as open to his father as he could possibly be. If a yawn opened and something ripped out of him, he was ready. He imagined the last moment of knowing; his father's life all but gone.

Yet what was at the core of him remained intact. John searched for something more—there had to be something more. What did he really feel?

His reaction was to build up the fire. Throwing on whole branches, he watched the flames leap. His father died. His father died. In deference to his father, he imagined the body coming home for the funeral: tears and wails, lives shattered —his mother's life shattered.

But for as much as he tried, nothing more came from him. John Henry didn't know what to think—for so long, this thing with his father had hung over him. Could he be beyond it? But where was that? The space inside him was alive, but in so many directions. In that sense, he was glad to feel the fire pressing against him—the flames outlined his whole body: his arms and legs, the tips of his ears.

The fire burned!

The heat was suddenly inside his clothes!

He leapt to his feet, slapping at his pants and shirt.

Even looking at the fire was too much and he stepped from the fire altogether.

John continued slapping at himself.

He stepped away, then stepped away further.

He shook his arms and legs.

The whole front of him glowed.

John continued shaking himself.

The heat in his clothes only gradually dissipated. He felt relief from the cool air around him.

John Henry stood with his back to the fire, facing the darkness.

His instinct was to just walk. He needed to get some distance. The pressure he felt from behind was more than the leaping flames.

John Henry took a couple of steps. The desire to get some distance continued. The direction of his life was to go forward. He took a couple more steps. From the light of the fire, he could make out the shapes of trees, but beyond that, the volume of the night was pressing. There was no doubt he wanted to walk, but how far? He would be walking in complete darkness. The idea of animals pushed against him. There definitely were bears and coyotes.

John Henry stood suspended. Looking up, he gave full attention to the magnificence in the sky. The stars were tremendous—there had to be millions.

He continued facing the night. The shapes and shadows of trees loomed around him.

Finally he turned around, stepped past the fire, and went back to sitting on the cooler. What he felt most was strange exhaustion. The remnants of the situation with his father lay scattered around him, but he felt no real need or opportunity.

What did he want? What did he want? Everything was up to him. He had things to eat in his cooler but he wasn't hungry. He would have a beer but not at this moment.

Mostly he was dominated by the idea of having the

whole night ahead of him. There wasn't anything he needed to do, and nothing else came to mind. He had plenty of time to think, but what about? He found himself in an odd situation. He sat looking around. It was just him and the night, and it would be a long time before he felt ready for sleep. Even the fire didn't offer much. Already he felt the fringes of boredom. He tossed on a couple of smaller branches just to keep the fire going. All he knew for sure was he was in for a long night.

A FURTHER VIEW

What a lovely memory. Coming back to me after all these years. From the far reaches of recollect, a true wonder of existence.

What could I have been but seven or eight years old, out in the schoolyard before the morning bell, all of us children staring up with outstretched arms into the wide-spreading branches of the great elm?

The memory offers a comfort. The world comes together, then drifts apart. Could the effort to focus completely dissipate me? What do I care? I have had my time.

All of us children spinning and twirling, yelling our joy with open arms beneath the wide-spreading branches of the great elm, as the last leaves of autumn, loosened by a brisk wind, come fluttering down to us.

Out in the schoolyard before the morning bell, all of us children staring up with outstretched arms, yelling our joy as the last leaves of autumn come fluttering down, spinning and twirling.

The dizzied glee of children, wind and leaves.

Such a perfect sense of release. Could this memory be my guide, as a beacon or an angel's hand? I have lived my life, with all its twists and turns, but now my time has come.

Out in the schoolyard before the morning bell, all of us children staring up into the wide-spreading branches of the great elm, yelling our joy with open arms, chasing the last leaves of autumn loosened by a brisk wind.

All of us children spinning and twirling. Yet the harder I try to stay focused on the image, the more scattered I become. Wind and leaves, the dizzied glee of children.

Out in the schoolyard before the morning bell, yelling our joy with open arms beneath the wide-spreading branches of the great elm, all of us children chasing the last leaves of autumn loosened by a brisk wind.

But the expanse moves, then moves again to become the curtains beyond my bed. Looking down, my feet rise in sweeps of whiteness. My hands lay scattered across a great plain as elements of a landscape.

How can I last the day? I might as well be resting in the sky. Each atom strains for release. Be gone, be gone, the universe sings a song. I have lived my life but now my time has come.

The joy of children with outstretched arms, chasing the last leaves of autumn loosened by a brisk wind.

But another memory appears, hovering on the periphery. And why not? What better way to spend my moments? Could the memory couch some further insight? No matter, the day stretches before me like eternity itself, and I will be glad if nothing else than to ensure against a boredom.

And such a different memory, released from a storage

that must be my cells. What could I have been but less than twenty? Yet so far beyond my life that I could hardly be alive. The world broke apart, and I had broken apart as well. What hell to pay for a young man with nothing to hold onto but a rifle.

Madness billows in clouds. I focus in then focus out. Horrors rise up. Yet it is not what I am after, and I make the effort to keep the images at bay. Something else is my source of intrigue. It was that other time of afterward, somewhere in between, the horrors of war behind me and nothing yet to replace them. Where was I? Nowhere to be found or coming back from far away? The war ended but what remained?

What makes me think I can answer anything? It is more than being oblivious that obscures my sight. My attention lies about like wisps of smoke. Yet I am curious. There is something to discover, or at least some feeling to embrace. To find a way, I urge my hands and they rise like leviathans from a frothy sea. I clasp them together, then to bring my focus further, push them closer. I have lived this life in flesh, so let its sensation be the horse I ride.

Returning to the States after the great war, I hired onto a truck hauling freight anywhere east of the Mississippi. The feeling is of whirls of motion, and motion was everything of what I wanted to become.

With the afternoon and evening off until my rig could be unloaded and loaded again, I walked out of the trucking yards of south Detroit and headed toward a river I had never seen but knew was there. What comes to me most is streets empty and drifting. March or early April, the spring rains had yet to come, and I remember being surrounded by a chalky grime, the same dust of demolished towns.

Where was everyone? How could a city be so bare? Continuing forward, my sense of direction began to flutter. Trapped to myself, I felt tilted toward a chasm. The chattering of machine guns churned the air. The sounds of explosions pressed against me. In the intense times of battle, my consciousness would separate, and I could have gone either way, toward living or just as easily to die.

Turning a corner, I found myself faced by scenes of industry. Hoisting machinery and the sound of jackhammers filled the air. Could I have been more relieved? There was a feeling of strength in activity. Walking past tableaus of construction, like witnessing a parade. The world was on the move, and I was on the move as well.

Did I smell the river first or sense the space? The streets left off and there it was, wide like heaven and cobalt blue! Hastening to the flow, I sensed the undertow beneath my feet, so if enough to open my shirt and set sail, I gladly would have been adrift.

And there were fishermen, in ones and twos, scattered along the shore. Just the sight of them thrilled my heart, and was surely a casting back to childhood days when all the wonder of the world could be contained in the catching of a fish. What were they catching, pickerel or trout? It hardly mattered. I walked the shore from several yards, to keep as many fishermen as possible in sight, anxious to see a silvery knot of muscle hoisted to the sun.

More than once a bell did ring, a rod did bend, and I turned in the direction, only to have all activity go slack as indication of a snag or something else. There had to be fish, the river's size and the old men's diligence guaranteed it. Yet as the afternoon shadows grew long and the wind turned cold, the fishermen one by one packed up and left the bank. I was not ready to leave. Something of myself had been cast upon the water and yet to be retrieved. On against the darkening air I walked, the motion of my legs my only solace.

If it were possible, I gladly would have spent the night, but a wind so bitter drove me from the shore. Unwilling to return the way I came, I continued further into town, fully aware I was traveling downstream. In a bar, I had a drink, in another a bite to eat. The image that comes to mind is of a body and a current tangled in a roll. My only definition an iced and winded outline, not so much wanting to enter but forced to go inside.

Even the woman's words at first didn't register. A cigarette or a light? My mind didn't work, as if something underwater. Yet the voice persisted, as if giving me chance to be polite. Once satisfied, she began to ask me questions. My first impression was she looked the reflection of life's hardship clear upon her face. But who was I to judge? Her eyes were bright, and as we continued talking, the life of a living person drifted to the surface.

She had come in from an outlying town and was heading east to a promise of work. It was her first time traveling. In that we were different, since traveling was all I knew, and she wanted to know about the road, the places I had been and all that I had seen. It felt good to tell her, my words unraveling from a private place, but no choice but to lead directly to the war. I was hesitant about the details but she persisted, even telling me of butchering hogs on a farm to convince me of her nerve. Why was she so interested? It was the first I had talked about such things. The bombs crashed again, the night split open and glints of steel flashed around me.

But she stayed solid as something to hold onto. We were young together, with all the world's power and uncertainty before us. What whiskey couldn't get us beyond, we laughed around, and even danced a couple of songs. By then we both had drunk enough. With nothing else but the world of men and women before us, we left to take a place.

Of all the women I have known, I have never felt such desperation to carve a hollow in the night. How good to feel the weight and substance of another living being. I remember fighting to stay awake against the current of sleep just to feel her skin against me.

Under different circumstances, we might have stayed together, though the light of day was harsh on both of us. I'm not sure how, but I came to think she wanted money for our time together when all she wanted was a couple of dollars to make her fare. Though the misunderstanding quickly cleared, the separateness between us continued through breakfast at a diner and afterward when I walked her to the station.

Taking a cab back to my loaded rig, the open road had always washed everything to even, but this time my edges would not erase. After several days of several states, I made my way south to my parents' place. I hadn't been back since returning from the war, though nothing much had changed. They were still hanging on to a farm they couldn't keep. The others had all gone, and I couldn't stay. Yet it felt good to uncover the blood between us. Ma was up before dawn to feed the chickens, then heaped stacks of cakes on the table. Pa and I walked together to the fields. It is the last memory I have of him, standing in his white sleeveless with his wide-spreading shoulders, silhouetted against the thick line of early-summer trees, staring across the corner field of freshly sprouting earth, speaking in that rich tone of his that contained the full weight and satisfaction of being alive: "The world can be green son, the world can be goddamn green!"

PETOLOGY: A PERSONAL HISTORY

Dwayne Pathis was one of those who continued their chosen course of study past college into a lifetime career. Yet he never had any particular interest in water management. The issue of water for Dwayne stemmed from wanting to contribute to the world, to be a part of the solution for making the world a better place. It became a matter of where he wanted to focus his life's effort. He needed to be involved with life beyond him; he felt his connection to mankind and greater existence; he wanted to be part of a real progress. And he wasn't comfortable with being an activist. Looking around, he saw how easy it was to be caught up in the issues of right and wrong, and how easy ideas pitted against each other ended up supporting each other.

What Dwayne liked about water was that it was essential, fundamental to life. It transcended the lines of human endeavor that might otherwise divide. If he could improve the situation of water, it would be for the benefit of all, to strengthen the core of their lives so they could be free to take on the greater challenge of being alive and human. The betterment of the world depended on the betterment of people. And the challenges of water were great. So much of the developing world did not have clean running water or adequate sewage treatment. After graduating from college, Dwayne joined an aid agency working in South America. The people he worked with were dedicated and achieved success. But there were factors of water he had never considered. Dwayne experienced water as a commodity of power that so often delineated a line between the haves and have-nots. It often became difficult to separate water from politics. Progress rarely proceeded in a straight line. One morning, he and the people he had been working with for more than two weeks to establish a well in a rural community woke to find that overnight the well had been filled in with rubble. Dwayne could be frustrated but he was also determined. When he finally did leave the agency, it wasn't because of any great loss of hope; he had tired of living in harsh conditions and from the realization that he would never get over the feeling of being a stranger in a strange land.

Back in the States, Dwayne took a job as the water manager for a small town in Virginia, and a couple of years later agreed to do the same job in a larger city for more money. A few years later, he was offered to be the water manager of an even bigger city. It made perfect sense; he was the water manager for the benefit of an even greater population; he could do more by doing the same. The increasing need for water conservation was always a foremost challenge. The need for updating systems constant. Technology was continually improving and had to be implemented. Money was always an issue. As the water manager, Dwayne was involved in budget battles, and of course, water was still often tied to politics; often, he felt his real job was as mediator between opposing views. Dwayne still considered himself a scientist, but he mostly managed antiquated infrastructure and was constantly preparing for breakdowns sure to come. However, his greatest management challenge could be dealing with staff. More than a dozen people worked in his department, and he interacted with personnel from other departments. Mostly, his colleagues were good people; he couldn't hope for better, but they could so easily get caught up in personality conflicts and petty disputes. It always amazed him how difficult it was for people to get out of their own way and just do their job. It meant that much of his time was spent managing personal pathologies, as the thing most difficult about his job. And he didn't think things could be much better somewhere else. People were people. It was just where his life had taken him. He had no regrets. Looking back at his life, he couldn't imagine doing anything different.

The thing he most felt compelled to do was to focus more on his own life. He wasn't exactly sure what that meant, but he needed his life to be bigger on his own terms. "It was time," was how he presented the situation to himself. He was making enough money; he didn't expect any great changes for the future, so there was opportunity. He needed his life to expand and extend. One of the things he decided was to get a pet. A pet would be for his own enjoyment, but also for his betterment. He wanted to feel connection beyond himself. Having a pet would definitely require commitment; it wasn't a decision he took lightly. Having a pet would make demands on him, but the rewards would be worth it. And there was little doubt what kind of pet he was interested in, he would get a pet vagina. A pet vagina offered him the greatest possibility. He knew what he was getting involved with; he had enough experience with vaginas and had been married briefly when he was younger. There would be challenges. He would have to be willing to adjust. But the world could open up to him. There was so much more to life that he wanted to experience. One thing was for sure: he wouldn't be hasty in choosing his new pet. He wanted his pet to have her own life, but not be too independent. He very much wanted her to enjoy being with him, but not be needy. He wanted someone who could take him places, but also wanted to be taken along. And he didn't need her to be a lot like him; he preferred if she weren't. He was seeking a fresh perspective, someone who could enrich his life and not merely fill a void.

After Dwayne began looking for a pet, it wasn't long before he met Sherri at a party given by someone in his department. They shared a drink, fell easily into conversation. She was professionally employed, seemed stable enough, and was easygoing. She was pleasingly plump and pleasantly pretty. They both enjoyed walks in the park and decided to meet the following Sunday. Their connection continued. They both appreciated a nature experience and being in open air; the azaleas were in bloom. The next week, they met for a movie and a few days afterward had dinner together. It was easy being with Sherri. She seemed open to life but wasn't adventurous. She seemed curious enough but not overly exuberant. She had been married before but didn't hold any grudges. Being with her was like walking out into open space. There wasn't any reason for them not to continue. They liked many of the same things; they both enjoyed cooking; he was intrigued by her interest in gardening. Before long, they were in the middle of something they had created. He had room in his house and she was only renting, so imagining them combining their resources became an adventure. When she finally did come to live with him, it seemed the most natural thing. Life was so much more when it was the two of them. They could be themselves yet add to each other. The world stepped back, and they stepped forward. It was the little things in life that took on greater meaning. They were a part of something wonderful to come home to.

It was during this time that Dwayne's balls fell off. It was disconcerting and something that would continue to dismay, but when he took time to think about it, the change couldn't be seen as any great need for restructuring. Balls were something most needed in greater leaps of faith, in efforts toward accomplishment and maneuvering, and he felt beyond all that. He had his disappointments, and his highest hopes seemed to have escaped him, but he had managed a good life. Sherri was consoling and supportive. It confirmed his feeling that intimacy was more a proximity of closeness, and the satisfaction of sex for him was greatest as a possibility, more powerful in the realm of fantasy and memory. He was pleased to believe his pet felt the same. It sealed their togetherness with a deep appreciation. He felt her grow more comfortable in her need to be with him, and they were definitely better as a whole; life together could be that good. For him, it meant that he had found enough, that there was so much less about the world he needed to be concerned about. They were life partners, and life was still a journey. It secured in him the understanding that he could live a million lives and never live the same life twice. There was a space around them that needed to be protected, and he would be diligent and strong. It gave her a foundation that allowed her to extend her feelings. Being with him gave her confidence and a sense of permission. His great joy was the feeling that she acknowledged what he had to offer. She made room to include him as her invitation for him to be involved, as if she wanted to return a favor, as if being with him could offer her some kind of boost. They might be out walking, and there would be the feeling of being at the edge of something great, looking out over an expanse, sitting along the edge of the great river, or staring up into the twisted branches of a large canopy of trees. She looked at him as if she had reached a point of wonder, as if the moment really was too much. "What a crazy place this is," she said, in a tone of amazement mixed with longing and maybe even a hint of anguish. "You come into this world. Then you have to leave it."

SAVING GRACE

Making his way through the streets before noon, the city is quiet on a Tuesday. Vehicles are limited, and the few people about amble absently in either direction. Dressed in his long robe, it is unavoidable to walk without raising dust. Already he is looking forward to returning to his residence and escaping the heat. He will have a quiet dinner before preparing for the committee meeting, and then afterward gather with members of the congregation for evening prayer.

Now he has an appointment to keep. It is his second meeting with the condemned. His schedule is to meet with the prisoner every second day before the event. He feels forced to admit a twinge of guilt for feeling some relief that the courts are swift in carrying out their decree. After a couple of meetings, there just isn't much more to talk about.

Reaching the gate of the prison, Clergyman waits to be let in and then makes his way down a long hallway. Pulling over a chair, he sits in front of the prisoner in his cell. Lucien acknowledges his presence by simply lifting his head from where he sits on a bed. The next moment, he gathers himself to stand and take a few steps forward. Pulling over a chair, Lucien sits, and the two men face each other through the bars of the cell.

Clergyman is careful that what he says doesn't imply Lucien's plight, but he wants to be able to offer comfort. It is understood that the condemned is not overly religious and has no close family. When he looks at his face, he is again struck by the leathery darkness of his skin. Lucien glances up at him with eyes reduced and hardened. "So how are they treating you?" Clergyman asks, expressing genuine concern. Lucien shrugs his shoulders, conveying that they, of course, aren't treating him well, but neither are they treating him badly. "Are you getting enough to eat?" Lucien nods that he is being adequately fed. "Are you cold at night?"

Clergyman has satisfied his interest in the proper care of the prisoner. But he has yet to find a way to address this man. Lucien is not forthcoming, is simple and contained. Even his crime seems to have been something beyond him. He was charged as a low-level member in a failed plot of conspiracy and sedition.

So he is surprised when he asks his next question and gets a response. The question is obligatory, and one asked at their first meeting when he couldn't even get a preference for a last meal. "Is there anything I can do for you?" With his elbows on his knees and looking over the darkness of his hands folded in front of him, Lucien lifts his head. "I would like it if my hands could be tied in front of me." Lucien's eyes meet him directly, in a clear desire to communicate serious intent.

After leaving the prison and on returning to his residence, Clergyman is left to ponder the request. For Lucien to even ask had surely required a bolstering of effort, the admitting of a need, as if he had gathered all strength to make an attempt. But is he aware of the difficulty? Though his request is simple, it is leaning against the great weight of protocol. Facing the gallows, the condemned's hands have always been tied behind. He can already hear the voice of objection. And he will be the one who will have to give reason. When he takes time to focus on Lucien's motives, he is forced to speculate.

A memory rises to offer comment on Lucien's interest. It is from something he read so long ago, he doesn't remember where. The article stated that of the number of suicides leaping from bridges over water, the vast majority of people jumped from the side facing land, versus the number of people who jumped facing the expanse of open water. As a seeker of insight into human nature and man's relationship to the divine, Clergyman found the results of the survey intriguing and was curious about the reasons given for the choice. He remembers it stated that even at their most desperate, the people choosing to face land perhaps found comfort in the familiar, and maybe some solace in a final connection to their fellow man. But what about those choosing the other side? He finds it a bit odd that he can't remember any of the reasons given. They must not have been satisfying, and he is forced to devise his own explanation. Did they choose to face the full force of the unknown as a way to abandon themselves to their true nature? Yet any higher fulfilling interest seemed negated by the act of choosing death itself. In relating the people leaping to Lucien's request, the most obvious difference was that the people deciding to jump were able to make a decision, while Lucien had no choice in his fate. And Lucien's interest seems to be more about a relationship with himself that lacks any connection with the greater world or the divine. With his hands tied in front of him, maybe he can clutch himself and be protective, rather than with his hands behind his back, feel his chest open and his heart exposed. Maybe the common element between the situations was a desire to seek simple comfort.

A matter of comfort is the foundation of what he offers people. He would like it to be more, and his hope is always to lead people to God and salvation, but offering comfort is where he lends most of his effort. It is his duty to advocate for the condemned. In Lucien's case, there is only one man who can grant such a request. Yet the mere thought of approaching the commander fills him with unease. The commander is crude, boorish, and completely uninteresting, with the great capacity to absorb the very air around him. Clergyman, however, has come to admit a kind of respect for the man. His situation is completely untenable. There is no hope of bringing peace to the region, and any order restored is either an exhaustion of the opposition or the balancing of powers destined to wobble again and become unhinged. The commander is condemned to forever live on an edge, constantly looking over his shoulder. He is either gallant in the face of insurmountable odds or ignorant and pompous to the truth. The saving grace of the commander is that he has avoided becoming completely mean or sadistic. He is a dedicated servant, which falls him to the fringe of being decent.

Sitting across from the commander at his large desk in his small office, he faces the hulking head with bulging eyes, framed by a drooping dark mustache and unruly hair that has resisted being forced in a singular direction. After delivering the request, all Clergyman can do is wait for a response. The commander stares at him, either annoyed or confused, though he is only at a loss by what he says next. "But why?" Then in the next moment, he dismisses any need for an answer. "Dead is dead," he states. Clergyman feels forced to nod his agreement, but before he can advance any further explanation, the commander interjects another line of thinking. "With his hands in front of him, he could use them. It could be a ploy. Cohorts could be plotting an escape?"

Clergyman cannot speak to the possibility of a plot. As for the condemned being able to raise his hands for some use, it is a valid concern. He has a simple solution. With the hands tied in front of him, they could also be tied at his waist.

The commander leans back, taking in what has been said. What Clergyman has going for him is that the commander is committed to working with him as the spiritual liaison between God and the prisoners. The commander's desire is to remain on the side of the divine.

When Clergyman returns to the prison to meet with the condemned again, he reports that he can't be sure but believes the request will be honored. Lucien responds by slightly nodding his head. Clergyman then initiates a prayer for peace and offers a tribute to the power that guides men's lives. When he asks if he can do anything else, he is surprised when Lucien states openly that he wishes he had done more to better his life.

On the day of execution, Clergyman takes his customary seat in the second row of the small group of people gathered before the gallows. He is generally relieved when the condemned is led in with his hands tied in front. When the mechanism triggers, he lowers his head and experiences a personal revolt against the tragedy of man, that true cruelty still happens, that against so much effort, the worst continues, that mothers are still destined to bury their sons.

North Dakota

Walking out the door and across the deck then down the steps his only interest as the best place possible as the place to have a chance walking across the backyard reaching the white fence before lifting his foot to the bottom plank and looking out even further over the fields and across the valley and past the rounded hills to where the power of storms seen billowing in clouds sweeping in sheets of rain and snow the lightning ripping sideways even the four twisters in his time snaking through the valley the cattle circling like figures on a carousel at the county fair.

And still no feeling of hint of indication or explanation or direction as any place to begin piecing back together from everything broke apart so that he is left stranded to some furthest distance because hope itself the very last thing to leave before reaching some limit as some kind of futility as some kind of exhaustion forced to relinquish as some kind of release the volume comes recoiling back at him until the only true reality of his son dragged down into deepest descent the full weight of eternity fallen upon him forever in a young girl hanging limp and desolate from a barn beam.

Is this my son? The same feeling after first hearing and racing around town to every possible place to any possible person who might know where and finding nothing to the point of madness as desperation he parked the truck to climb that hill in such long strides gasping for breath and even further before standing among the other declarations before stepping to his son's lettering as tall as him slapped and splashed in blue paint over scraggly vegetation and rocky ground to spell out ML + TS and off to the side and below the overlapping TLA understood as *True Love Always.*

Is this my son? In all the effort and determination in slashing brush strokes to proclaim a greatest feeling of love and promise in reaching for something to base a life upon professing to the world so that in a further attempt to understand he turned from the hill to look out over the town spreading silent and inert as the backdrop to a young girl as shy as she was pretty hanging from a barn rafter until feeling that same desperation he hurried off that hill to again race around town before getting the call that his son had returned and racing to meet his wife with such wildness in her eyes pleading at him against his own momentum to not rush their son at least their son was safe she holding onto him until them spinning around across the kitchen together her promising to deliver their son just give her a chance her woman's knowledge and power forcing him to concede.

She leaving across the room the hallway to the bedroom and him trailing enough to hear her pleading and cajoling through the door in such soft and loving tones as to a young boy like he hadn't heard in years until in more practical terms him retreating to the back door to both hear her placating but also for the sound of the window opening if their son tried to escape then hearing nothing believing contact had been made she would have their son in her arms knowing he would have his chance he walked out the back-door and down the steps.

Still he waits against the volume beyond him against the volume of the world undone against anything even possible having no resemblance whatsoever to anything imagined or even recognized so when the back door does open and he does turn to the vaguely familiar as still his son their eyes meet an instant before he turns to walk the length of fence his son coming down the steps angling across the yard to where the fence ends and the fields meet to across the valley beyond to the rounded hills to God and Jesus and all the saints he having to come up with something as all his life has ever been and forever will be.

HEY HEY PAULA

When she first saw the woman, she didn't know it was a woman at all, and passed with the rest of the people who flowed around the three of them, collecting bottles from the crowd. It always amazed her to see bums on the streets, and she stared transfixed at their worn and dirty clothes. Then the realization struck her—it was blood! The dark stains on the back of the pants were blood! And before she realized, she said "Daddy!" with such shock and urgency that her father had been shocked himself, and quickly asked her what it was. But she couldn't tell him, and when asked again, she just refused. The crowd rushed her along. The hot air dizzied her. As soon as they got inside the stadium, she told her father she needed to use the bathroom.

Still she sits in the bathroom. From inside the stall, she can hear the anxious chatter of women and from the space beneath the door, she can see the bright light reflected on the tile floor. The heavy queer feeling is still with her. She had never seen a woman bum before. Yet the woman's face was not like a woman's at all and was grotesque like a man's.

And the woman had bled all over herself. She could not imagine a woman bleeding all over herself.

She stays inside the stall until sitting alone on the toilet is the last place she wants to be. Finally she stands and breathes deep to make herself strong, then opens the door and walks directly out. When she leaves the bathroom, her father is waiting for her. "What took you?" he asks, both alarmed and annoyed.

She does not say anything. She only wants to walk. "Are you alright?" her father asks, but she is already past him.

She only wants to walk. She starts out fast but slows down to walk with her father. Around her, people move in all directions.

When her father takes her hand, she lets him. It is a feeling like falling back, and she lets it happen. Her father leads as people stream around. When he turns down a long ramp, she can see bright sunshine at the end of the tunnel, and just as they come into the open, the crowd stands and cheers wildly. In front of her is the wide-stretching field, luminous and glowing, and across the expanse of green grass the players in their bright uniforms fan out, running to take their positions.

POSTCARD TO WHERE I'VE BEEN

I have always been impressed by how quickly I said yes when Drew invited me to accompany her on a business trip to Taipei. What was I thinking? Obviously, I wasn't. It was as if something poised inside me uncoiled, and my hand sprang up, like a volunteer answering a request. And I never had even the slightest interest in going back to Taiwan. Sure, my time there had been of great significance, but that was more than eight years ago; nothing had been left undone, there were no regrets. And I had my own life to feel good about. Most importantly, a beautiful daughter, a satisfying career, and a future I believed in. I'm sure I wouldn't have had the same response if the trip were to a place like Spain or South America.

After my initial reaction, I did step back from the invite; I couldn't just leave, even if it was only for a week or so. But Kate was turning five, and my mom would be glad to help; she always wanted to spend more time with her granddaughter. Being on a business trip, Drew had a hotel room paid for, and her allotted meal stipend would be enough for us both to share, so all I would need to purchase was a plane ticket. As soon as I presented the idea, my mom was only excited, and I recognized her vicarious thrill for me whenever some opportunity to enhance my life became available. There was work to deal with, and I had been nervous about bringing up the idea of a trip because of company policy against taking time off on short notice. But they were only supportive and believed I had worked hard and was due a vacation. It confirmed the feeling that I made the right decision working for a smaller firm.

The trip became a matter of details. The biggest challenge was coordinating my flight schedule and seating arrangement with Drew. Otherwise, I had to update my passport, stock up on groceries for while I was gone. I even got out a pocketbook of Chinese translation from a box in the back of my closet and made an effort to brush up on Mandarin, with little hope because the language was so difficult and I had such little success before, but it would be nice to feel at least I could be functional.

When Drew picked me up for the drive to the airport, we clutched forearms and squealed like schoolgirls. I'm not sure we stopped talking the entire three-hour flight to Denver. We had met in a weekly Pilates class that didn't offer much opportunity for personal interaction and had gotten together for coffee a couple of times. Still, we had never really gotten to know each other. It was interesting to learn about her growing up in Missouri and attending a rival college.

The next leg of our journey was a much longer flight to Japan. Having talked ourselves into exhaustion earlier, we settled into a personal strategy of passing time reading the books and magazines we had brought along. It was my first experience with in-flight movies, and I believed any desire for distraction could easily be satisfied, but encountered the odd effect of watching movies I couldn't get interested in, making me even more aware of myself.

What rescued us from absolute boredom was the scenery out the window. We had assumed flying direct to Tokyo, the path of flight would be over ocean, but suddenly we were experiencing an expanse of complete snow, great rolling mountains and deep sweeping valleys. We could hardly believe what we were seeing. Stretching for hundreds, perhaps thousands of miles, there wasn't a town or dwelling or even a road visible; not a single sign of man. I thought I understood wilderness but this redefined anything I had imagined. We had to be flying over Alaska or the Arctic. Just when we felt saturated by immensity and beauty, the plane lifted up to reveal a whole other kind of whiteness rolling out below us to the horizon. We drifted above a sea of clouds undulating in waves beneath an endless blue sky. When the plane turned, we were treated to a brilliant sunset, increasing in flaming color until the horizon spread orange and red, before fading through a full gradation, diffusing to complete darkness.

Seeing the lights of the Japanese coast was a revelation, mostly for the promise of moving my body. Departing the plane, we were definitely in a foreign country, but with enough English around to be familiar, in the signs, in the kinds of fast-food restaurants, and in the presence of other Westerners. With a layover of more than two hours, we tried to get some sleep, but the configuration of terminal seating made it impossible to get comfortable. We were glad to board our next flight, as it brought us closer to our destination, but we knew the nine-hour flight would be tough. It happened in complete darkness. It went on and on. We felt we had entered the life of the condemned. Beyond distraction, we struggled in a strategy of personal survival. Faced with such a long duration, we finally felt compelled to engage with each other and commit to conversation.

Drew admitted to an apprehension about the trip. Even though she had traveled abroad with her company before, this would be her first time as team leader, with people she would be responsible for, working in collaboration with a Taiwanese company to develop a manufacturing and distribution strategy for IT components. It was a big deal. There would be negotiations. Her biggest concern was in dealing with the Chinese. Over the last weeks, she had been through cultural training, but knew nothing could fully prepare her for face-to-face. The Chinese had a reputation for being ruthless, cunning, and even devious. She feared their attempt to take advantage of her inexperience and being in unfamiliar surroundings. Having lived in the country, she was anxious to hear my impressions. I had never been in a business situation in Taiwan, but believed, like most people, the Chinese would press for advantage if only to ensure their position. Otherwise, my impression of the people of Taiwan was that they could be determined and diligent, but I also found them to be genuine and direct, as well as bright and optimistic. I saw her biggest challenge as being female in a very chauvinistic society, but believed that to be the challenge of almost anywhere.

Our conversation made it clear to me what Drew's interest was in having me along. I had thought, having lived in Taipei, my role was to help Drew expand her visitor experience, to help her mix business with some pleasure. I now understood her need for moral support, to have someone outside her work to talk to and spend time with, as a kind of buffer, a counterbalance, a pressure release.

The rest of the trip became a particular kind of hell. The best hope was a state of retreat. Any awareness of the self became a soreness. Physical discomfort became blaring to the point of acute pain. I felt I was able to glimpse the edges of insanity.

Finally we arrived. It was like lifting up from a stupor. We shuffled off the plane with the others, only to face the long lines of customs. What I first noticed was a different kind of foreignness, a complete absence of anything English or familiar. Without another Westerner in sight, as two white women in a sea of Asians, we were glaringly conspicuous. I had been through this before, but had no memory of any similar reaction. I took the awareness as testimony to having been younger, oblivious, with little understanding of issues and all that could go wrong. I now felt my concerns reflected in Drew, who seemed to stiffen and lean against me. I felt forced to bolster both of us. Once through customs, we made our way out of the terminal to the bus that would take us to the transfer station.

What hit me was a jolting memory of the smell of Taipei. Even though we were still miles from the city, the smell of diesel, mixed with grime and a dank tropical humidity, was so pungent and pervasive, I was immediately transported to full awareness of a city dense and complicated. After giving an attendant the white card prepared by Drew's office with proper instructions, we found our bus and were soon lurching through the dead of night. Along the side of the road were deserted shells of roadside stands and bare-bones shops, and up in the darkness, faint lights of dwellings scattered throughout the night gave dimension to high hills. Soon the line of squatty buildings on each side of the road merged to continuous, as the efforts of people making a living on the fringe of the big city. The stream of buildings steadily increased in height and depth until becoming a volume pressed against the road. Reaching the main station, we handed another card with the name and address of our hotel to a taxi driver. Soon we were being driven through streets filled with mass and bright lights and taller buildings. Even at three in the morning, there were plenty of cars and people walking. Arriving at our Western-style high-rise hotel, in a cluster of similarly modern hotels, we were only relieved. The familiarity continued as we walked through the door into a spacious lobby, similar to any we might find anywhere in the States, with high ceiling, marble-tiled floor and plenty of dark wood. Walking up to the expansive length of the reception desk, we were greeted by a very professional-looking attendant, dressed in uniform with a welcoming smile, who spoke perfect English.

Riding the elevator to the sixth floor and entering our room, we were more than pleased. Our room was as big as an apartment with high ceilings and full-length windows, and a bathroom bigger than either of ours back home! Relief washed over us as we both fell backward on the king-sized bed. We were halfway around the world! We had to be exhausted, and after getting out of our clothes, we were quick to get under the covers and turn out the lights. But after lying a while, we were surprised at not feeling close to sleep. After another period of lying there, we got up and took time to unpack and organize the bathroom, before properly washing our faces and brushing our teeth. Getting back into bed, Drew especially needed to sleep; she was due to at least make an appearance at work later in the day. But sleep wasn't happening. After another stretch of trying, we felt forced to admit we might have fallen victim to the dreaded jet lag, that strange phenomenon of disturbed equilibrium that can be the scourge of long-distance travelers. We both had some experience with jet lag and knew it was possible, but jet lag didn't always occur and varied from person to person, so we hadn't wanted to give it any real credence. In truth, it was six o'clock in the morning and six in the evening back home so it was little wonder sleep was screwed up. By then it was daybreak. Pulling back the curtain, we could see hotels similar to ours rising before us. Turning on the TV, we couldn't find anything in English. The decision then was whether to get something to eat; the hotel served continental breakfast, but it meant getting dressed again, and Drew's concern was possibly meeting someone she knew from work. Finally, we both took showers. With nothing left to do, we lay back down.

The bedside phone rings and we both jump. Our first thought was that we had made too much noise and someone complained to the desk. The phone keeps ringing. It is decided Drew should answer since the room is registered in her name, so I hand it to her. "Hello." I watch her face as a look of concern quickly spreads. "Are you sure?" Drew turns to me with eyes widening. "I didn't think until this afternoon?" Her eyes open to complete panic. *What the fuck!*

What the fuck! she mouths at me. She ends up shaking her head in an attempt to clear it. "Can you give me ten minutes?" She then hands the phone back and I hang up. "What the fuck!" she exclaims, her voice escalating to complete dismay, "She's here to pick me up! She says I was supposed to be ready at seven-thirty!" We both look at the clock. That's exactly the time. "No one said anything to me!" Surely there has been a miscommunication. Drew continues in the throes of panic. "Are they messin' with me? Are they messin' with me?" she asks, referring to her perception of what the Chinese are capable of. I don't have an answer, but I feel the need to offer support. "Can you be ready?" Drew is devastated. "I have to."

Drew jumps out of bed to become a kind of whirlwind, throwing on clothes and rushing to put on makeup. I stand by ready to help. Drew fixes her hair. The last thing she decides is what shoes to wear and asks my opinion. Removing items from her briefcase, she gathers her laptop. She steps to the mirror for one last check of herself and is out the door.

The maelstrom has lifted. The room becomes suddenly quiet. Half expecting Drew to return, having forgotten something, I am left with the feeling of a rough day ahead for her.

But I am also aware of being alone in the room. It is a bit of a shock. I am back in Taipei. I lived here.

The shock continues. My thoughts can go in different directions but I hold back. There is still the issue of needing sleep, but for the time being, I have lost all hope. As a sort of default, I turn on the TV, but a quick scan through the channels confirms nothing of interest.

Stepping to the window and again pulling back the

curtain reveals a brighter daylight. Down below, people walk the sidewalks. The two buildings as other hotels, rise before me to dominate the landscape. When I take time to look past them far to the right, I can see another kind of building as part of a line of familiar buildings, as the kind of buildings that make up a neighborhood, the two and three-story cement apartment buildings connected and continuous for blocks and blocks, that are the bulk of the housing stock in the city. Living in such neighborhoods is how I spent my time in Taipei. I feel a tug of nostalgia, but also a feeling of relief that the proximity to neighborhoods will give Drew and me easy access to the everyday of the city, something of interest to both of us. But for me, the presence of the neighborhoods has more immediate meaning. With the whole day ahead, they offer an option. I hardly expected such possibility so soon, but am faced with the growing awareness of nothing to do. Boredom is imminent. That frazzled feeling of definite jet lag covers my skin.

I am not anxious to venture out. It doesn't mean I have to go far. It would feel good just to look around. I putter about until the decision has been made for me. I dress in comfortable clothes, then double-check to make sure I have passport and room key. Reaching the elevator, I ride down and exit the lobby.

Immediately, I am engulfed by the sound and motion of rush hour traffic, streaming along the boulevard past the line of ragged palm trees just steps in front of me. The volume is affronting and shockingly familiar, especially the whining of accelerated scooters—I am reminded that Taipei is a city of over a million scooters. That familiar smell of exhaust mixed with pungent tropical humidity! As soon as I reach the sidewalk, I turn right and walk past a continuous line of scooters and bikes parked perpendicular along the road. For the moment, I am trapped in din and motion. Reaching the next corner, I turn right again, propelled by a need for relief. Immediately, the traffic lessens, and I walk along a side street stretching between the looming hulks of the Western hotels. Up ahead, I see the line of buildings that got my attention earlier from the window of our hotel room.

At the next corner, I turn right and am now walking parallel to the face of the apartment buildings. Traffic remains light. Immediately I feel greeted by evidence of neighborhood life: food carts parked at the end of alleys that serve as the thoroughfares through the neighborhoods. The memory jumps at me. The carts appear every morning to serve breakfast to schoolchildren and people on their way to work. How often I had a cup of hot peanut soy milk or a fried egg with scallions sandwich, always on white bread cut diagonally.

The glimpse into neighborhood life is intriguing. I am on the verge of something palpable. Not feeling I have reached a limit, I also don't feel any simple way forward. At the next alley, I cross the street and stand at the corner. Because of the curve of the alley, I can't see much into the neighborhood, but I am very familiar with the high cement walls on either side that form a narrow passage. Faced with a reaction of concern, I remember how safe it felt as a Western woman walking the streets of Taipei, with its minimal street crime and little police presence. As further comfort, the few people who pass by me give little notice.

Poised before making a choice, I finally venture into the alleyway and feel pressed by the buildings. I pass the steel gates of entrances to flats and apartments, and above me on second and third floors, scattered along the walls, jut small balconies stuffed with plants and personal items. I am reminded of the density of Chinese living.

What next catches my attention is the sight of mostly older women and men walking past me, carrying bags or baskets with flowers or the tops of leafy vegetables sticking out, indicating an outdoor market nearby—an essential feature of neighborhood life. It is a delight to think I might see one again. How often I went to such markets! They came up in mornings and were gone by afternoon. As I reach the intersection to another alley, more people walk toward me carrying evidence of market and I turn in the direction. At the entrance to the next alley, I see even more people. As I make the turn, I feel faced with the concern of not wanting to lose my sense of direction, but what gives me confidence is the realization that if I ever did feel turned around, I could make my way out of the neighborhood and get a taxi.

At the next corner, the flow of people to the right has increased to a steady stream, and up ahead, I do see colored umbrellas on either side of the alley above the crowd. There is the market! I open to the experience. Making my way, the crowd swells to a throng condensed to a few feet across as I start with the others past the umbrellas. Underneath spreads a continuous patchwork of blankets and carpets with baskets and boxes, small stacked shelves displaying all kinds of fruits and vegetables, nuts and herbs and various wares. I see bright yellow starfruit and ruby water pears, orange papaya, bunches of leafy bok choy and nappa cabbage. And clusters of leche! I hadn't thought of it in years! That strange and exotic fruit I nearly lived off and bought in bunches, each the size of a walnut with leathery nodular skin peeled to reveal a translucent and juicy fruit like a skinned grape, sweet with a hint of sour.

The banter of buying and selling swirls around me, and I look closely at the vendors with their wizened faces and wide-brimmed hats, dressed in their traditional loose pants and shirts or blouses, as I wander past displays of textiles and trinkets alongside herbs and twisted roots, next to baskets of small dried fish heaped up like silver dollars. Reaching the intersection of another alley, I look past a different flow of people, to another sight I recognize, a tin roof stretching over the alley as indication of an entrance to a more permanent market, also common to neighborhoods. Drawn by the promise of another direction to explore, I turn and join the crowd. Entering the market is like entering a dim tunnel. My focus is to stay walking on a curving pathway of pallets and uneven boards. To either side small stalls and booths of different-size walls and configurations are covered with burlap and blankets, that separate the space into individual rooms that are lighted but staggered, to form an off-and-on brightness that shines up from the rooms to both illuminate and shadow a shared raised ceiling of tin sheets and corrugated steel, cobbled together overhead to form a continuous roof extending above the entire market. I am struck by the organic nature of something grown up on its own. How was it ever decided that an alley for travel should be closed off to traffic? The air is moist and heavy from the periodic rain that must leak in, and is thick with the smell of incense mixed with cooking. The real intrigue is the individual stalls, each a small world of different goods. One room is filled with household items of pots and pans, gadgets and utensils. Another room is filled with jars of teas and spices, while the next is filled with religious items, including statues and prints, as well as displays of incense.

The further I proceed, the more dominant is the smell of cooking, until ahead I can see a larger area opening to a kind of food court, hazed in smoke and low light. To my right, lining the wall are raised displays of mostly pre-made and ready-to-eat items, including various meats, rice and bean mixtures, and tofu products formed into shapes and combinations, stacked and piled up in divided but continuous sections. Down the middle of the open space stretches a line of small booths and kiosks, each with sizzling woks and steaming pots of boiling oil in front of a small counter with a couple of stools. Amidst the dim light and shadows, rising steam and heavy smoke, customers choose to mix and match from a variety of food options, prepared to order with chosen sauce and spices.

The lively atmosphere of people talking and pointing, with the thick smells of food and smoke, is like walking through a dim cavern. The volume is continuous. Faced with the choice of entering another passage to another section of market or an opening to the outside, I choose the need for fresh air. Walking into the light of day is a relief, and again I am in a narrow alley with high walls, with more people selling wares displayed on the ground on blankets. But the activity isn't as intense and seems to be a side arm of the market, with vendors only intermittent. I would like to find a bench or chair, but there are none. I am not interested in going further. Finding an empty space on the wall, I lean back against it and after another moment, slide down to sit

on my heels. After another moment I sit on the ground altogether, pull up my knees and lower my head.

Taipei was a place across the world, exotic, with the promise
of adventure. There were people I knew and people they
knew and people we met, all traveling to explore. I chose
France as my starting point because I studied French in both
high school and college. After France, I traveled to Italy and
then Portugal. Taiwan became an option when my latest best
friend had a friend who knew someone who was leaving a
lease. Arrangements were made, but Alesha became ill and
had to return to the States just before going. Money had been
paid, a plane ticket purchased. There was talk of others
coming, but it came down to only me. I was nervous and
uncertain, but meeting people had always been easy. I felt
the need to expand myself. Mostly, I believed the world
believed in me.

I never accounted for the language barrier. Everywhere I
had been, English had been prevalent enough to get by, but
in Taipei, the foreignness was dense and complete. My
inability to communicate was debilitating. The very core of
my existence felt threatened. My shock only continued when
I found my apartment no bigger than a cell of ceiling-to-
floor cement, a single fluorescent light above a dresser and
mattress of who knows what, and a community bath. That
first night, I huddled to myself, unable to sleep from the
sound of heavy traffic echoing directly down the open stair-
well to my room, and being bitten repeatedly by what
seemed to be the same few mosquitoes. Most disconcerting
was realizing what it could take to get out of this place. The

immediate challenge was just to feed myself. Taipei was massive and strange. Being white and female became a terror. My saving grace was a block from my apartment, I found a 7-11 convenience store, similar to the kind found everywhere in the States, but unlike any 7-11 I had ever experienced. I managed to locate crackers, juice, and strings of cheese. My big concern was that I might miss my contact, surely due to arrive any moment. When I tried calling the number from the community phone, I was always greeted by a different person who didn't understand the name "Peter," no matter how many different ways I pronounced it.

Not until the following day did he arrive, and then he only seemed to be satisfying some obligation to check on me. He was older, thin and frazzled. When he seemed anxious to leave, I would have assaulted him if he hadn't answered my questions. He told me where I could find a bank to exchange money, but the best information he provided was directions to a Buddhist cafeteria, which he thought would be my best chance for food. In the serving bins laid out in display, I recognized egg in some dishes, and by scooping a portion onto a plate and taking it to the counter and after having it weighed, held out my hand for the cashier to take the proper amount of money.

The cafeteria is where I met Molly and Christine, a gay couple from Australia. Unlike the few Westerners I had seen who didn't seem anxious to meet me, the ladies recognized my plight, and after learning they came to the cafeteria most afternoons, I planned my dinners then. The women were near thirty and had lived in Taipei for six years. What I came to understand was that, unlike the Westerners I had experienced in other countries who were mostly passing through in a spirit of adventure, people coming to Taipei mostly worked and lived in the city. The women had no plans for leaving. But as I came to know them, there was something reserved and retreated. They clung to each other as all they had, as if they had been chased to the ends of the earth and were making their last stand. But I was grateful for their willingness to acknowledge me. They told me of other places Westerners frequented that I might be interested in, but the best information offered was a lead in finding work. The ladies knew of a German guy giving up his position tutoring school kids and put me in touch. After meeting with the parents, what most impressed them was English being my native language. I started immediately and met the four children aged nine through twelve, after school, in a courtyard of one of the family flats. My only requirement was that all conversations with the children had to be in English. Otherwise, I could take the children wherever I chose, which was a great way to learn the city. We visited parks, museums and numerous shops. The only other condition was that I had to have the children returned home by six-thirty. I was given money for expense, but for refreshment could only buy something to drink.

Most impressive was that the few hours a week I worked paid enough to sustain me. I became familiar with various cafes and places to eat, but what truly caught my attention was a bar the ladies mentioned as a place where Westerners often hung out. The bar turned out to be dark and edgy. Just walking through the doors and being washed over by the punk grunge of Iggy Pop was a huge relief. The crowds were mostly on weekends, and I did meet people and even got invited to parties. But I never received the kind of reaction expected. As one of the few Western women, I thought I would get more attention from the men. I had always considered myself attractive enough with lively personality, and even though enough of the guys were interested in spending time with me, the bulk of their intrigue was reserved for Asian women. And I could hardly blame them. Asian women could be such wonders of exotica with their slender bodies, angular faces, glistening black hair and porcelain-like skin. By comparison, I could feel gangly and thick, and I had never felt that way before.

And the Asian women were just as intrigued by the Western men. It was a true attraction of other. And because of their fascination but lack of experience, the women lacked any ability to discern. Many times, I saw some gorgeous creature with a guy I wouldn't have given the time of day. And the men were well aware. More than once, I received a knowing smile, communicating the understanding that the guy knew he wouldn't have a chance with me, but had found something so much better, and could hardly believe his good fortune, and that the joke was on me. And the attraction didn't work the other way between Asian men and Western women. I felt their interest, but they were either too shy or intimidated and ended up being overly polite. I attributed their response to being raised in a chauvinistic society where women were demure, and not knowing how to react to someone direct and assertive. It made me feel destined to a lonely future, but I was determined to make the best of my situation and decided to cultivate a deeper relationship with myself. I decorated my apartment with wall art and artifacts and started practicing meditation.

I met Jen Min at one of the weekend parties held by

Westerners and recognized him as one of the Asian guys who hung around at the fringes, either connected to the group by a degree of friendship or business contact. Jen Min didn't speak great English but spoke very good French! He had lived in France for three years and studied at university. How good it was to be speaking French again! We both had spent time in Paris but preferred the countryside. We shared a love of food, hanging out in cafes and riding bicycles. But he became disappointed when asking about my time in Taipei and heard I hadn't had a great experience. He took my impressions personally and was quick to come to the defense of his city, being sure I just hadn't had the right opportunity, and offered to show me some alternatives. I felt fortunate for the chance. Being the beginning of the weekend, it was decided we would start the next day. We met at my place and took a series of buses to the city's outskirts to visit the National Art Museum, a massive structure of white granite and several floors, each divided into rooms designating different periods and art forms. There were sections of tapestry, calligraphy, painting and sculpture, and one entire floor dedicated to fantastic displays of the most elaborate and intricately carved jade artifacts and sculptures, dating back thousands of years. Even with his great pride and desire for me to see and experience everything, Jen Min held back his direction and comments. We were often together yet also apart, exploring different rooms, only to eventually find each other. It made our time relaxed and fun. We agreed we didn't have to see everything and eventually cut our touring short and retraced our steps back into the city, where he directed me to a tiny restaurant where I first encountered those wonderful dumplings stuffed with meat or vegetable and steamed or fried, delivered by the dozen in covered wicker baskets, served with a variety of sauces as well as condiments of pickled cabbage and turnips and sides of tender baby greens, sautéed in garlic and butter and washed down with cold beer.

The next weekend, we continued our excursion at a large outdoor park on a brilliant sunny day. We sat in a grandstand with hundreds of other people cheering wildly as teams of half a dozen men in brightly colored uniforms paddled furiously in long boats, fronted with carved heads of fierce dragons on long, sweeping necks, and raced up and down a wide river. On another trip because of my new interest in jade, Jen Min took me to an international market beneath a highway overpass with stretches of tables as long as a football field displaying all kinds of jade artifacts and antiquities, and the thin circular bracelets of every color and gradation that Chinese women wore as the traditional "bangle". Another time we visited a park of at least a hundred banzai trees, the size of a person, decades old and planted in rows, each meticulously sculpted and manicured. After all our excursions, there was plenty of food. Taipei could be seen as a city of eating, especially in the evenings when whole outdoor sections of streets came alive with booths, kiosks and food carts gathered together, preparing and serving. I often had no idea what I was eating, but trusted Jen Min, and always experienced something surprising and delicious.

But my real entrance into Chinese culture was reserved for tea. Tea was a way of life for Jen Min, the center of his heritage and passion, as well as the foundation of his family's business, and the reason he had lived in France and studied at university, to learn modern business practices. For me, tea had never been more than a breakfast alternative to coffee, though I was vaguely aware of its greater importance in places like England and Japan. But for the Chinese, it was essential to everyday life and had ramifications extending beyond social into an element of spiritual and religious. Taiwan was a nation of Buddhism and Taoism, with the observation and study of nature an essential avenue of awareness and insight. For well over a hundred years, Jen Min's family grew and distributed tea from the family farm in the rural interior of Taiwan. Jen Min, as the eventual successor, had been charged with updating the business for modern times with a focus on further expansion into international markets. It was why he needed to live in the big city and have a small office. I was surprised to realize there were establishments throughout the city dedicated to the experience of tea. The tea houses were always quiet places with a subdued elegance of mostly natural light and dark wood that exuded a feeling of reverence, like walking into a chapel. The space inside was divided into private places of booths and tables where people came together in an intimate setting and spoke in soft tones.

Once inside the tea house, we would be delivered by attendant to our seats and offered steaming hot towels to cleanse our hands. After making our selection, a tray containing the components for making tea was delivered. The drinking of tea for the Chinese was deliberate but loosely structured, and had the casual tone of close acquaintances getting together, unlike what I thought of as the Japanese tea ceremony, which in contrast, seemed ritualistic and ceremonial.

What struck me first was the size of the teacups! They

weren't much bigger than a thimble and seemed as delicate as eggshell. The teapot itself was miniature and could easily fit in the palm of my hand! Together, the porcelain cups and tiny clay pot hardly seemed functional. The teacups were placed first in a larger ceramic bowl and poured over with boiling water to purify. They were then set aside, and the pot with tea was placed in the bowl and filled with hot water, then drenched to "wake it up", infusing the porous clay of the pot from both inside and outside with heat to release the essence of tea infused into the pot from years of use.

The teapots were absolute wonders. They could be fifty years old and made from select clays from different regions and had distinct properties. The pots varied slightly in size and shape, particular to place of origin, and varied in color from dark, earthy tones to reddish brown. Each pot was dedicated to a certain kind of tea. It took years of interaction between tea and hot water to properly season a pot. Over the years, the pots developed a depth and luster of burnished wood that radiated an inner glow. The clay pots were prized possessions and each tea house cultivated a collection.

After the first pouring of hot water, the tea was allowed to steep to cleanse it of any impurities. The pot was then poured off into the bowl and again filled with steaming water. When ready, the tea was poured into the tiny porcelain cups.

The first tasting of tea was often light and airy, evoking a rush of impressions of fresh bloom, fragrance and emerging growth. After experiencing the full extent of the first pouring, the remnants of tea from both the pot and the cups were discarded into the bowl, and the pot was again filled with hot water.

The change in taste between the first and second pouring of tea could be dramatic. After the initial feeling of chasing after hints and glimpses, the elements of the tea in the second pouring began to expand and separate into different components and distinguish themselves in scope and character. True qualities began to emerge. A power of connection was made. Images and impressions of nature were most conjured, and I could be transported to deep forest or high meadow and be dominated by the imprint of blossom and rich bloom.

The dinking of tea was a call to contemplation and insight. There could be emotion and imagination, flights of fancy. For the Chinese, drinking tea was centered in an experience with natural elements, patterns, dynamics, most notably experienced in cycles, the change of seasons, the progression of day toward night, the development of youth toward maturity. As the simplest of acts, the drinking of tea revealed a connection to mystery and wonder, inspired by change, as the only true constant, the source and foundation of all creation.

The evolution of tea unfolded over several pourings, each tasting unique, highlighting emergence and complexity and revealing its true nature. The tea would weaken toward the end, often revealing its deepest character as a singular expression.

I left the drinking of tea exalted and satisfied. All I ever wanted was a depth to living, an avenue to greater life, a chance to experience the full scope of possibility. My idea of Jen Min had been dominated by my notion of limitation between myself and an Asian man, but here was a man of depth and caring and keen sensibility. I was a woman of desires. We moved into each other's arms, anxious to abandon to the full power of man and woman, to a depth of connection and pleasure in the thing we created, only wanting to go there, as our new definition, the feeling of jumping off only to climb again, to a place beyond precedence, lost to a feeling of leading but also of being led.

We spent most of our nights together. Jen Min's flat was larger than my apartment, with a much nicer view. Breakfast in the mornings became an adventure of fruits and pastries, and of course, tea. The only demand of me was to meet the children after school. Jen Min began taking me on his trips through the city to make contact with his network of distributors and exporters. At times, we visited warehouses and would be up to our elbows in tin bins of tea the size of small barrels, sampling for taste and texture, aroma and the tightness of leaves. My favorite place to visit was a small building that housed the transfer of the magical clay pots, sold mostly to tea houses. On shelves in rows sat pots in full display of every possible size and shape, and gradation of earthy color. Each pot was a work of art reflecting a heritage of great craftsmanship, testimony to the legacy of apprentice and master.

And everywhere we went, Jen Min was greeted by people happy to see him. So often we would be brought into some back room to be shown something special or treated to prized tea. And Jen Min never hesitated to include me. It was understood we were together, as a couple, without ever a feeling of me being flaunted. Aware of his connections to the community, that word of him being involved with a Western woman had surely reached his family, I never felt him falter. He felt willing to stake his claim, be his own person, live his destiny, as testament to what we had together. It made me look to an expanding horizon, fresh and exotic. How far could it go? When I looked at where I had been, I found a collection of bits and fragments and general impressions of a life lived, inherited, not really chosen.

On weekends, we extended our excursions further out from the city. We visited a series of Buddhist temples, solemn and serene, tucked against hills and seeming as old as time itself, reeking of deep silence and contemplation. Another time we traveled to a bathhouse fed by mountain streams, and I remember being submerged to my chin in a room clouded with steam, watching disembodied figures draped in white drift suspended.

Our furthest trip was by train far into the countryside to a distant village, where we would spend the night. What caught my attention was the severity of the landscape. I had known Taiwan to be a country of steep hills and tropical vegetation, but what I encountered went beyond anything imagined. Rugged mountains rose to jagged peaks that fell into deep gorges of rushing rivers. Around every corner across every bridge, a dramatic scene of beauty and desolation unfolded. The effect became cumulative until I held my breath. Every human attempt to come to terms with raw wilderness seemed feeble and precarious. I felt I was witnessing complete domination. After nearly a full day of travel, we reached the village nestled deep in a valley. I felt myself clamoring to understand how and why the place even existed. Against the forces surrounding its very destiny seemed undermined. Yet the village became the picture of quaint and idyllic. The people were calm and friendly, exuded optimism and content.

We walked the streets and visited the shops of artisans and purveyors, experienced the focus of good work and dedication. That evening, we had dinner in a restaurant of three tables. As darkness settled, we shared tea in the smallest of cafes. After returning to our simplest of rooms, we made love as celebration and a desire to exhaust ourselves. That night, I experienced a restless sleep, feeling the pressure of either a looming volume or a pressing dread. In the morning, I was relieved to see daylight at the edges of the window, and stepping forth, pulled back the curtain to face a staggering sight. Several feet beyond and from far below my feet, rising to high above me, a wall of lush tropical vegetation glistened glowing green. The immensity rushed my heart. My breath suspended. My only hope of relief was in a beautiful naked man sleeping, bathed in sunlight. Such a scream rose in me that I leaped upon him, had to have my mouth on him as the only avenue of direction, but kept falling until all the way through, never reaching an answer but knowing the question was too much to even ask.

THE COUNTRY CAR

In single file they walk the fence row. The taller one leads, his shotgun hanging from one hand at his side, pointing forward as he walks head down and serious as if tracking an animal. Several steps behind the other comes, his shotgun cradled into the crook of his elbow, supported at the butt by his hand so the barrel points past his shoulder into the sky. He too walks with his head down but without intensity or direction, just a lazy slump that keeps visible beneath the bill of his hat the steady, methodic conquering of his brother's boots marching through the mud.

At the end of the field, the taller one stops and takes off his hat to wipe his forehead. He stares up at the sun with eyes squinted, then steps to the wire fence dividing the two fields. The other comes and takes the shotgun handed him. The taller one then presses down with both hands on the top strand of barbwire and swings one leg over. Straddling the fence, he hesitates a moment, then punching down at the barbed wire, snaps his other leg over in a swift arc, like releasing tension from a double-bent spring. The other hands over both shotguns and climbs the fence. The taller one hands back a gun before starting off and resetting the tandem between them.

A short way down the fence row the taller one comes to a stop where humped yellow grass juts out in a bend into the gray field barren with corn stubble. The other comes and stops a few feet behind, staring with the taller one across the empty field at the white house glaring from a yard of scattered farm things.

"Dad's still home," the other states.

"So," says the taller one, his voice decided and fatal. He turns, faces into the curved peninsula of brush and raises the shotgun.

"Blam! Blam!"

The taller one remains sighting along the barrel. The day is shattered of sun, air, leaving just the earth pinned beneath his aim.

Lowering the gun like snapping off a tree branch, he walks with long strides straight down the line of fire, never taking his eyes off the stack of tires lying against the fence, half hidden in the tall grass. Crouching in front of the faded gray rubber, he lifts a hand to the faces. Along the front, the tires are peppered with small, jagged dents, cuts, and with his forefinger the taller one visits the fresh black holes, digging in his nail, gouging out small pieces of rubber. He then takes a couple of steps back, his eyes gone black, inspecting the line of tires. Turning on his heels, he walks off, stiff and straight with his head down past his brother. The other puts his shotgun back in the cradle of his arm and follows toward the house.

In the middle of the fields, or in one of the middles of

fields that wash off in all directions, having only as focal points tiny houses that struggle to anchor the land to a fixed position, is the small yard of the old farm. It is a rectangular yard of roughly two acres with a white house and dilapidated barn sitting in precarious balance at the diagonals. The barn is ancient and looming, sway-backed almost to collapse, weathered as ash-gray soil after final plowing. Around it lies scattered the discarded implements of farm life: disc plow, rolls of rusted barbwire, crippled tractor bowed to one knee. Across from the barn sits the white house, dressed in faded aluminum. It is the second house and sits a short distance from the crumbled ridge of stone remaining from the homestead.

Behind the house, just off the driveway, lies the car. There are other cars back in the yard but they lie in tall grass like sleeping dogs. This is the car. Like a deadly beast, it looks both terrible and striking, lying poised near the house, displayed in death. Smashed patches of glass hang jagged around the windshield, the hood and side panels are horribly buckled, with the twisted front curling back in a vicious snarl. Against the immensity of a quiet land, the car flashes mag wheels, a sleek back feline and fast. It is the center-piece, the fulcrum between barn and house, the axis spinning a gray land on a badge of violence.

The two brothers walk bent forward with open coats flapping against arms, like crows fighting a wind. They follow the fence row to the back of the yard and then cut an angle for the house. The taller one is in front and stares past the wrecked car, like cutting a path for his body. The car has its face quartering away across the driveway, yet the taller one strikes his gaze in a confrontation of wills that leaves both objects dead even. The other is again several yards behind his brother. He too feels the pressure of the car as he makes his way to the house and walks with his head down watching his brother's boots passing one at a time from beneath the bill of his hat, knowing his brother's gaze, knowing the fight that is going on, the fight that is beyond him. The two brothers reach the house and step onto the porch. The taller one pushes open the door and they enter the breezeway.

At table sits the father. At the stove stands the mother. The father lifts just his eyes from his plate and listens to the entering of his two sons. The shooting in the field has come to the house as announcement, and the father braces his gaze for his sons' entrance, then decides better of it and returns to his eating. Seated at table, he is a big man with full cheeks and a strong chin that ties in his other features to form a sturdy workman's face. His dark, full hair is tossed back off his forehead, his eyes stare gray and cloudy into his plate as he listens to the movements in the foyer.

With his boots off, the taller one enters and walks through the kitchen to peer over his mother's shoulder into the frying pan. The mother stands with her back to the kitchen. She is a sturdy woman of sturdy strength, gained from a long lineage of homing a sturdy land, moving against sturdy animals. She feels her son over her shoulder and offers him a view of the frying meat. Her hair is long and dark, streaked with gray strands, drawn back and pinned to lie against her. She wears no apron but has brown slacks and a green sweatshirt.

The other son comes and leans against the kitchen doorway. The father looks up from his plate.

"How'd ya do?"

"Got two," the son answers directly.

"Shot 'em good I hope," the mother says in scrutiny over her shoulder.

"Oh yeah. Head mostly."

He slips off his brown hunting coat, reaches into the back game pocket, and fishes around a moment before, with one long sweep of his arm, he draws out a rabbit by the hind legs. The mother glances at the rabbit. The son then steps over and reaches into the taller one's jacket hanging in the doorway, drawing out the second rabbit, holding them both in front of him in display.

The father looks carefully at both rabbits: the stiff legs, the matted fur, the brownish purple blood on the faces— evidence they have been dead a while. He then stares fixedly at his taller son standing in profile behind his mother, offering only the strong line of his jaw.

The father had warned his son of shooting into the pile of tires. It had become a strange ritual for his son to empty his gun before coming to the house. There wasn't anything terribly wrong about what he was doing; the boy bought his own shells. It just seemed unnatural, a strange cruelty that left the father uneasy. He had talked to the son about not shooting, and used as reason the many rocks around and the tires themselves that might ricochet back the pellets. The boy had taken in every word with a cocked, discerning stare until the father felt as if he was cajoling a small boy to not go near pigs because they'd surely grab him and eat him for supper. The shooting never did stop and the father was forced to change his reason to: "Because I said so." Since then, it seemed all the rabbits of the fields had come to live in that small plot of grass surrounding the tires and the boys had killed, or at least shot at a rabbit each time they went out.

"You shot those this morning," the father says into the middle of his two sons, making it clear he knows the two shots he heard had nothing to do with the dead rabbits.

The remark splits the kitchen into four separate units. The other son drops his eyes and walks the rabbits into the breezeway. The taller son remains standing behind his mother, watching his dinner fry, his face set in the haughty defiance of refusing under any circumstances to confess.

The father goes back to eating while watching his tall son. It seems they have been fighting each other a long time. It is a fight that came forward slowly, as an exercise between a father's will and a son's growing up, and in that the fight was expected. But the fight kept growing, like a pot boiling until now the father can't put the lid on or find the flame. But he's not going to avoid the fight either. This is still his house. The time will come for him and his son, but it isn't now.

And this other son that doesn't fight, that knows nothing of fighting, that somehow has had the ability to fight stolen from him. What of this son? And the father thinks of the two sons combined. He thinks of how each is a different half of what was and how that half has nurtured until it has become something more, yet something terribly unbalanced. And the father thinks of what had been that other whole and dares not give it a name. Out of hope for his two sons, he swore against it, and has tried to let that name float away from him out into the fields, not so that it was gone, but so it would become wide and not so heavy. But the name has stayed, and the father felt it rise over this house until he knew and yes, would even say to himself, "Was the cause of so much." The father called it "dead son." That was all the name he would give it. He had promised the fields he had given the spirit of his son to, promised the spirit of his father, the spirit of his ancestry plowed beneath him into the land.

The mother brings dinner to the table and the two sons sit down. The father watches them both, heads down, begin working at their plates. His sons. His two sons.

After finishing dinner, the father goes to his room and prepares for work. A heavy melancholy has begun to settle over him, so by the time he is ready to leave, he is in a surly mood. The father walks back into the kitchen to get his thermos and lunch pail. The two sons remain eating with their heads down. His wife stands over the stove. And suddenly he is a stranger in his own house—his own house! He gathers his things and is glad to leave.

"I'm off," he tosses into the room.

The father enters the breezeway. On the floor lie the two rabbits, stretched side by side. He glances at the bloodied faces, the rumpled bodies.

"And have these damn rabbits taken care of!"

Along the straight road cutting a thin line through the wide fields, comes the lone figure of a girl pedaling a bicycle. She is an older girl, in that awkward age when features of womanhood are easy to predict but still demand a fair amount of projection. Her chin would surely sharpen, her eyes would learn to dominate the face, and the sharp angles of her thin body would temper to finer sweeps of line. As it is, she is a dark-haired girl, tall, with a strong face high-lighted by dark eyebrows under which stare clear brown eyes. She will be a striking woman, not a real beauty, but a woman who is ardent, commanding, and the lighter of fires among men.

Down the road toward the girl comes a car. It appears nothing more than a shiny bar in the middle of the road. With a discerning stare, the girl watches the car's coming while pumping the pedals, listening to the hiss of tires cutting through the loose dirt. A sense of confrontation arises between these two lone objects moving toward each other down a thin line through the wide fields; a dangerous insistence that surrounded by all this emptiness, each should have room enough to be left alone.

The girl watches the car grow bigger then pedals to one side, preparing for it to pass. Lifting her head, she gives a slight smile toward the windshield, punctuated by a quick lifting of her hand.

With the woosh of the car passing, the girl looks down again. "I'm leaving," she says, just loud enough for herself to hear. "I'm leaving."

And so it is done with her father. The girl stands up on the bike and works the pedals hard against the road. She feels important to herself and stares off across the fields, feeling the dull earth in its infinite flatness echo her importance as the lone flower, the center of movement, the hub of these fields washing up around her.

As the girl nears home, she looks over the place where she has lived. It seems so different now, like she has already been gone and is first returning. She looks hard at the thin bare-patched lawn, the rutted driveway, the jumble of fenders, drum barrels, slat wood scattered around the aluminum white house jutting from the disarray. And like someone no longer belonging, the girl allows herself to judge; to judge the people who live here, the people who will someday die here. It seems a waste, such a waste. The girl judges it all finally with a quick sneer. She is leaving. "I'm leaving."

The girl turns into the driveway and the car comes to her. It lies along the back of the house yet the girl knows its crushed face, the jagged hole of a windshield. She gets off her bike, leans it against the house and walks around to the door at the back. The car leers hideously. The girl hates the car. She hates what belongs to it, hates her father for not getting rid of it when she asked. With her eyes averted, the girl jumps over the two steps onto the porch and enters the door.

The mother turns from the sink, giving the girl a sharp frown to show her entry hasn't gone unnoticed. At the table the two brothers sit, starting to clean rabbits. The girl bends down to undo her new sneakers. The shoes are splattered with mud. Her mother had told her not to wear them but she wanted to; it had been important this morning, so she had worn the shoes.

The girl stands up and moves into the kitchen. On the table, one rabbit lies purple-fleshed and naked, sticky with blood and loose hair and missing its legs and head. The taller brother has the other rabbit in his hands and pulls the fur from the middle of the back in both directions. Like an obstinate child, the rabbit fights its undressing, fights the coarse hands that don't soothe or make quiet before starting their business. The brother pulls hard at the fur, showing his teeth clenched in effort, and the rabbit gives in with a long, fresh ripping sound as the skin forms shirt and pants pulled over the head, down off the purple haunches.

"There, just gotta pull harder," the taller one states, handing the rabbit back to his brother.

The girl, disgusted with bloodied hands and meek rabbits, moves past the table to the mother working over a stack of dishes in the sink. The girl leans against the refrigerator, absently watching the cloth of the woman's sweatshirt rippling across her back.

"Where you been all this time?" the mother asks, chastising the girl with her back turned

"Just visiting."

"Visiting?" the mother retorts. "I'm getting tired of this visiting. You'd think while there's no school you could make dinner with your Pa. He works hard ya know."

The girl lets the words flail at her. Waiting for her mother to continue, she listens to the hollow clapping of the dinner plates. She will take no dinner. The mother says nothing more, and having waited long enough, the girl turns and goes to her room.

For more than an hour, the girl stays in her room. Lying on her bed, a great weight drawn from the room itself descends upon her, leaving her to struggle with her past and all the rest of her life. It had never seemed much of a decision to leave, and when the time came, she said "yes" with the same cool embrace of a woman accepting flowers. It isn't much of a decision now either and the girl brings the struggle to herself, letting the might and fury of her will fight head-on with the sum total of what life might bring her.

When tired of the conflict, the girl simply concentrates on a handsome young man with flowing hair and a rich, furtive face. There she lies, feeling the low flame stir in her belly and then rise, catching and spreading through her limbs until her body blazes with a strong fire of finality.

With a quick flick of her eyes, the girl gets up and leaves the room.

"Where's Tom?" she asks her mother, seated in the living room watching television.

"How should I know?" the mother returns in her usual tone of bother.

The girl passes on through the kitchen to the window. The first place she looks, she finds her brother out back by the barn, sitting on the old rusted tractor in his oversized coat. It is a familiar place. A twinge of pain drives against the girl, the first real pain she has felt this whole day; the same pain she always feels when seeing the desolate figure of her brother lost to thought in the small field of a greater land. Her poor brother. Her poor brother. Many times, she has watched him from her bedroom window. He seemed so frail to the girl, so helpless as to cause her heart to ache so strongly she begged the gods of living come take her, do with her what they would. She was strong enough, deserved enough, to have fate leave its handprint on her heart but spare her innocent brother, who brought no quarrel to this world.

And so the girl goes to her brother. She rarely went near him when he was like this, usually choosing to love him fiercely from a distance, but today she needs to be near him.

In the late afternoon, the sky remains full of sunlight but has lost all its heat and intensity, casting across the earth a thick mixture of shadow and sunshine. Closing the door behind her, the girl wraps her arms across the front of her blue sweater and moves off the porch. In the grass lies the car. The girl refuses it, holding her breath in a slight inhale as she moves her legs past its crushed front while staring out into the backyard at her brother, silhouetted against the great barn, leaning forward with his arms folded on the tractor's steering wheel.

"Hi Tom," she calls softly as she approaches.

The boy turns and smiles faintly then turns back to the bare fields.

The girl comes and stands next to her brother. This is new to her, something she knew about but never dared enter. She turns, leans backward against the great gray tire and stares across the wide, sullen land. There is no need to look at her brother. She knows his body, but knows none of him that drifts away and is scattered to the fields with the sweeps of wind. It is this she has come for and must go to meet in the middle of the fields.

"It's not that warm yet," the girl says, casting her words out with the breeze.

"You cold?" returns to her.

"No, not really."

The girl feels comfortable enough, having warmed up to her brother just beyond her back. She has always loved her brother, mostly from afar, but now she has come for him, to be near him for a while.

"So whatcha gonna do Tom?" she finally asks, the words rising up in her.

"Whatcha mean?" comes back to her from the fields.

"You're gonna have to do something."

With that, she turns and looks up at her brother, and he meets her gaze with eyes as pure as an animal's, a cow's or a fish's; having no instinct to demand anything, no need to get an equal share.

Her brother shifts back from the steering wheel and stares into the fields. "Yeah," he finally sighs. "I know."

"You gonna stay here?" she asks, feeling an urgency to press the issue.

The girl's insistence makes the brother uneasy. He leans forward in the tractor's seat. "I don't know," he answers. "I'd like to have these fields back someday."

"To farm?"

"Yeah, I'd like a farm."

The girl turns and sweeps her gaze across the land then looks to her side at the sagging barn, weather-worn and empty. It all seems horrible. She has always seen living here as just horrible, with so much not included—these dead farm things with their cinnamon-and-nails smell of rust, the dank odor of rotting wood, the frozen steering wheels she drove and yanked on as a child. Now in her brother's face, she can see another vision of this place, a vision of fertility and peace. Yet it is the dull ache of disdain in her stomach as she stares over the rusted cars and past the great dead barn that seems endlessly more real.

"Tom, you ever been in love?" she suddenly asks, the words escaping out from her before she has time to think.

Tom turns, breaking into a quick astonished laugh. "Now what kind of question is that?" he asks in amazement, his trance with the fields cut off right at his face.

" I don't know," the girl says, becoming embarrassed but glad to have her brother all to herself. "I was just wondering."

Tom turns back to the fields.

"Well have you?" she persists, a seriousness welling up in her.

Tom remains staring out as if waiting for his words to gallop in from the fields.

"I don't know," he says finally.

The girl looks into the side of her brother's face. A dark cloud has gathered on his brow and he is thinking, not just letting things pass into and out from him anymore—he is thinking. He belongs to neither the girl nor the fields now but is trapped finally in the web of his own living.

The girl is crushed. In the awkward silence that follows, she knows the mockery of her question, she knows what she has done. She knew the answer all along — she knew it! The question wasn't for Tom it was for herself!

Yet the question was for Tom! It was to save him! To tell him about the world beyond this place. There is so much she wants to tell him. She's in love! She is! And it could save Tom. She knows it and wants to tell him of the power of feeling, the thrill and joy and how much she comes alive. She wants to tell him. Tom. Her poor brother Tom!

The girl lies limp against the tractor so that when the return question comes, she fears it.

"You ever been in love?" Tom asks with a wry grin, trying to capture some of the question's original spontaneity.

The girl turns and leans back against the great tire. "I don't know," she replies flatly, staring at the huge shell of the barn. Her answer is a lie, determined to reconcile her separateness with her brother.

"C'mon, what about this boy we been hearing about?" Tom questions, hoping to tease her.

"I don't know," echoes the girl.

.   .   .

In the night the girl lies awake in bed, waiting for the house to sink deep into emptiness. It is done. It is done. Finally the night comes as thick, dark liquid, without dimension of walls and roof; a wide sea the girl floats under in a slow, dreamy current. She gets up as if the current has stirred the bottom of the sea. Already dressed, and putting on her jacket and taking her backpack, the girl glides effortlessly to the window, opening it without a sound. A gentle wind moves to take her and she feels with relief its coolness across her face. Quietly she slides one leg up into the window opening, then the other, and with a quick push, drops lightly to the ground.

The drop jars her insides. Now it is for real. She suddenly feels herself being nowhere at all, in the middle of some huge space she has to cross. She starts along the wall of the house toward her bike.

Off the corner of the house lies the car. The girl had been aware of it the moment she leaned out the window, and now as she nears the car, it looks from the rear like a shadowed bulk crouched in the dark, letting the girl pass easily. But from the front, it is a deadly thing, and as the girl steps in front, she glances at it before offering the car her back. In the dim light dancing across metal the car leers. Its smashed windshield and crushed front sparkle a strange language of flickers and shimmers the girl understands only with her skin. Turning the corner, she shivers in the cold, feeling the car's gaze bored into her back.

It is a burden to move now. Stepping to her bike she gets on. In the dim light flooding the driveway, the girl is exposed and pumps her legs hard, if only to reach the darkness.

On the road the girl feels better wrapped in the cold black of night. She can easily make out the road as a lighter shade of dark stretching away beneath her and feels safe listening to the tires slicing through the crisp mud. She has so long to go; this road seems so long now. She thinks of the morning. She thinks of a beautiful sun. She thinks of the big tree up ahead that will mark her entrance.

Far ahead a car turns onto the road. Immediately the girl knows who it is—it is her father! Coming home from work! In a panic she begins pumping her legs, staring at the twin moons burning toward her through the dark. She pumps furiously. But she can't make it. She won't! The car is still a way off, but how far? Can the lights reach her?

When the girl dares to go no further, she turns to the shoulder of the road, slams on the brakes and tumbles into the tall weeds. Scrambling to her knees, she drags the bike off the road but is immediately met by thick brush. Leaving the bike where it is, she fights her way forward. Fear of discovery explodes in her chest as she flails desperately through the branches. But after a couple of feet, she runs into the field fence. It is too late to climb it, and jumping to a tree presses her back against the trunk.

The girl presses against the tree, feeling the pounding of her heart. To her side she can see the lights growing in the road. Quickly she looks for a bigger tree but seeing none, presses herself even harder against the trunk and braces herself, listening to the increasing mechanical hum of the car as it approaches.

The car passes in a heavy rush. The red taillights retreat in a steady flight through the night.

The girl steps from behind the tree, staring after the

fading red. She wipes her hands on her pants and brushes herself off. Stepping to the bike, it is an effort to pull it back onto the road, but she does, then gets on and starts pedaling.

From the dark shadows lining the road, the girl can make out the wide arms of the big tree up ahead. She continues to pedal fast, and when she is almost up to the tree, a tall figure steps boldly out from behind it into the road. The figure gets closer, its legs spread firmly apart, the hands shoved into the pockets. She slows down and jumps from the bike, running the last few steps to meet him.

"That was your dad," he states in the night.

"I know," the girl says, searching for his face.

The figure takes the bike and moves it off the road. The girl follows as he lays the bike in the weeds behind the big tree. As she nears, a hand comes to her, first on her arm then moving to meet her own hand. Another hand comes and the two hands help her over the fence. The figure climbs the fence and jumps to the ground beside her. A hand again comes from the darkness and finds her hand, and the girl runs beside him over the field through the night.

A GOOD LONG
AND WIDE

The opening of the front door catches his attention, and as he continues working, he listens through the whine of the needle to the movement in the shop. By the soft shuffling on the bare wood floor, he already knows it isn't either of his partners. Besides, they're both finished for the afternoon. It can only mean one thing, a customer. A customer. It's the last thing he wants. He hoped the design he was working on would be his last of the day and he could get off early himself. Oh well, it doesn't mean they want anything.

It takes a while, but finally from the creaking of the floor, he can tell the person is approaching the entrance to his office. He becomes very intent in his work and is aware of the doorway only out of the corner of his eye. When the person steps into the opening, he doesn't shift his gaze.

"How's it goin'?" comes the young male voice.

Bill flicks his eyes in the direction— "Be with ya in a minute"—then returns to his work.

Yet in that instant the person is familiar. Only after a moment does he realize it, and by then the guy has already moved out of the doorway. More than anything else, the dark hair was recognizable: full in front and swept across the forehead. Then it comes to him and he reacts with surprise. Yeah, it was that kid. That's exactly who it is. And Bill hadn't expected to see him again.

The picture clears in his mind and Bill finds himself smiling. The incident was one of those unusual situations that happen sometimes in the tattoo business. They all have their stories. Heck, his partner once had a woman have 666 tattooed on a spot shaved on her head as some kind of leverage, if needed to shock her old man when he came home from the service. Weird stuff.

And the kid's request had been almost that unusual. As Bill remembers, it had been about this time of day, just before closing, and since he was with a customer, he thought one of his partners would take care of the guy. But he specifically asked to see Wild Bill. Recommendations always gave Bill a secret thrill, especially in front of his partners, since he considered himself the best tattoo artist around. So when he was available, he took care of the kid and made the effort to be friendly. And right away, it was obvious the kid was a little unsure about what he wanted, so Bill directed him back to his office. Even then the kid didn't have an easy time explaining, but finally said he wanted the tattoo to be of a woman's torso, cropped at the waist and neck, and below the elbows. It didn't make any difference to Bill. Only then did the kid say he wanted the torso to be his girlfriend's.

By then Bill was starting to get a kick out of the kid. There definitely was an off-center quality about him: unsure and a little shy, but wearing a black leather jacket and faded jeans that went with his haircut to give him that rude-boy look that was popular. And there was a wild-eyed quality to him that became more apparent the more comfortable he became. Getting his request out in the open, the kid became animated, to the point of tracing in the air with his fingers and hands, trying to make Bill get the picture of what he wanted.

The distinguishing detail of the torso had to be the breasts. It was what would make the figure specific. The kid's girlfriend's breasts were very unique. It was an effort for Bill to both give his full attention and keep a straight face, but at least it wasn't the usual skulls and hearts and stuff. Okay, let's talk about breasts. He had surely done enough women's breasts before, so he doubted he would have any problem.

Bill showed the kid all the different breasts on his stencils and on the designs on the walls, and when that didn't work, he even got out his sketch pad and tried to bring what the kid was describing to paper. But nothing was exact enough. It was decided the breasts were round and they had some upturn, and they weren't big or small, but the unique factor was the nipple area. The whole nipple area was supposed to be sort of swollen. Bill wasn't sure he had seen that kind of breast before. They weren't having any luck. And it was partly because he was intrigued that he finally suggested it might be best if the kid brought in a photograph. Immediately, the kid seemed to deflate. It was as if the image in his head suddenly didn't seem possible. Bill thought the idea of a photograph was a good idea and tried to encourage him and even went so far as to bring out the photo album of his work to convince the kid he was good at freehand, but the kid didn't regain his enthusiasm. When he left the shop, Bill very much believed it was the last he would see of him.

Now that the kid is in the other room, Bill's intrigue has quickly returned. It is the kind of thing that for him gives tattooing its flavor.

As Bill puts on the final lines of the leading paws of a ferocious tiger, leaping out from the bicep of the man he is working on, he finds himself having to struggle to concentrate. When he is finished, he is even more relieved than usual.

"There you go," Bill says, in a tone of crescendo.

For the first time in a long time, the bearded, burly guy in the chair looks over at his arm. He flexes it a little, inspecting the tattoo. "Well goddamn!"

The measure of satisfaction in his voice pleases Bill. It does look good. "Now you'll be the big cat on the block."

As the man gets up and stretches, and Bill gives the information for the care and healing of the tattoo—the guy has other tattoos and is surely familiar with everything being said, but it is a note of professionalism that Bill is very conscious about—he moves over to the doorway to let the kid know he is finished. When the customer steps forward, Bill decides to lead to the front and make it look official by being paid at the register.

The kid is still there, looking over the tattoo designs that cover the walls.

Bill is also suddenly aware of someone else. It happens when he is talking directly to the customer in front of him, so he only notices the figure out of the corner of his eye, and by the time he has a chance to look, he is already hoping. Sure enough, it is a young woman sitting with her hands in her lap on the bench along the wall. A further wave of intrigue washes through him, yet he is suddenly aware of not wanting to be obvious. Still talking with the customer, he doesn't look again. When he walks behind the length of counter to the register, she is out of sight.

The guy pays him the agreed-upon price plus a ten-dollar tip and Bill thanks him, again saying he hopes the guy enjoys the tattoo. The guy is sure he will. Before he walks out, they share a quick nod of appreciation and a last cordial smile.

Alone now, Bill takes a moment to gather himself. Another situation is ahead of him.

Walking from behind the counter and strolling down its length, Bill stops when he reaches the open area. The kid turns from looking over the walls and smiles. "How's it goin'?"

Bill nods, "Not bad." He then turns to the woman on the bench and smiles and gives another quick nod. She meets his eyes for an instant and smiles herself. She's decent-looking. With her gold-brown hair brushed back and her somewhat shy yet open gaze, there is a brightness about her. She has lively eyes and a soft, roundish face.

The kid is already at her side. "Jan, this is Wild Bill."

Again they meet eyes and smile, and again Bill nods.

But the introduction has also made him conscious of himself and he runs his fingers through his long hair, then with his thumb and forefinger traces down the edges of his full mustache. The three of them facing each other threatens to cause an awkward silence. Bill takes the lead. "So, what can I do for ya?"

The kid hesitates. "Well I was here a week ago…"

Bill nods his head, letting the kid know he recognizes him.

The kid pauses. "We talked about doing a tattoo…"

Again, Bill nods in acknowledgment.

The kid shrugs, looking over at the girl. She remains calmly looking forward. "Well I'm still interested."

Bill is also interested, and his reaction is to invite the two of them into his office. With an outstretched hand, he directs the way. The guy waits for the girl to go first, then follows.

With only two chairs in the office, Bill grabs a third chair from the office of a partner and sets it next to the other chair facing his desk. The two of them sit down and he sits down at his chair across from them. It causes more of a separation between the three of them than he would like but what can he do?

As the two of them get settled, Bill takes the opportunity to look them over more closely. He has already decided he likes the woman. Seeing her move and then sit down has given her a fullness—there is a nice feel about her; she carries herself well for being young; there is a slight unsureness but at least she doesn't compensate for it by acting tough. She's slim but not thin, with a nice shape. And Bill liked the embroidery on the back of her jean jacket. He didn't get a good look but it was a large radiating design, dominated by oranges and yellows. Otherwise, she is dressed in black jeans and white sneakers.

Seeing them sitting together offers a new perspective: They look all right together, different, but there is the feeling that they are a couple. It makes Bill look at the kid differently. He has to admit his first overall impression was that the kid was a little…well, flaky…a little "out there." It was his almost hyperness that most gave that impression, but seeing him now, Bill doesn't feel it as much. He now finds that grin of his, that is continually brought back to a smirk, appealing. The kid is wearing the same leather jacket but now it seems to fit him. Bill guesses he is in his early twenties.

Leaning back from the edge of the desk, Bill raises both arms and brings his hands together behind his head. "So you want a tattoo," he starts, getting their attention. "And last time we weren't having much luck."

The kid grins and looks down, shaking his head. The girl has obviously been told about the first meeting and smiles herself. Bill is glad to have caused such a reaction.

"So did you bring a picture?"

Again, the two of them have a shared reaction, though they don't look at each other. They shift in their seats then shift back. All along Bill has been aware of that kind of awareness between them.

The kid looks at him. "We were wondering about something else."

Okay, he is open to anything.

"We were wondering if maybe the real thing might be better."

Bill has to bite down so as not to show a reaction. They both are watching him. He nods his head; yes, he can see their point.

"You see it really means a lot to me," the kid starts in a sudden spurt. "It's really important that this comes out right."

Bill hurries to the kid's aid. He knows just where he is

coming from. "Hey tattoos are for keeps. You gotta be sure. It's nothing to be taken lightly."

The kid registers relief and Bill is relieved.

All along, the presence of the woman added up to this as a possibility; it seemed far-fetched but did offer a solution. And for the first time, Bill lets himself believe it might really happen. Staring at a pair of breasts while inking a tattoo isn't a bad thing.

A silence develops. This time the decision isn't up to Bill; he can only wait. The kid leans forward, thinking a moment, his hands folded in front of him, his elbows on his knees. The woman is sitting motionless next to him. Bill is suddenly conscious of not looking at her.

"So you think you can do it?" the kid asks.

Do it? Yeah, it will be freehand and that's a challenge. He is ready to convince them of his ability.

"You think you could do a sketch first?"

"Absolutely!" Bill answers emphatically. He wouldn't consider doing something like this without doing a sketch first. He even lets a little indignation slip into his voice as if his professionalism was being questioned. The kid simply shrugs, saying he didn't know.

Still, a decision has to be made. The kid goes back to thinking, but Bill gets the feeling that most of his attention is on the girl. She remains motionless in her chair as if what is going on doesn't concern her.

"It really means a lot," the kid reiterates. "I need this to be right."

Bill is quick to assure his complete understanding and agreement. He then goes on to promote his confidence and ability to do freehand.

Finally, the kid leans back and sighs. "Okay, let's at least try a sketch."

The decision causes a stir among them. Bill reacts by turning his back and reaching for a sketch pad from a desk drawer, then walking to them has the two of them get out of the chairs. Bill arranges a chair for the woman and takes the other chair for himself, moving it to a few feet in front of her.

All the while, the moment of undressing looms between them. Bill mostly feels uncomfortable for the woman, so when it occurs to him to lock the front door of the shop, he immediately tells the two of them of his intention and excuses himself.

But by the time he reaches the front door and locks it and hangs the "Closed" sign, another feeling has begun to overtake him. He has to ask himself if he really knows what he is getting into. This isn't his usual kind of work. Freehand isn't easy. Can he be getting in over his head? The fact that he even questions himself causes him to falter. Is it false pride that makes him think he can handle this, or could he just be getting caught up in wanting to see a pair of tits? Word of a bad mistake could get around. There's the kid to consider.

Walking back to his office, Bill has decided he still hasn't made up his mind. He keeps telling himself that he is only doing a sketch. He can back out afterward.

When he enters the room, the girl is seated with her shirt off, with the guy standing next to her. There is a moment of uneasiness but they all treat it as no big deal. Taking the sketch pad Bill sits down.

Immediately he notices that the light has to be shifted and getting up, he moves to take care of it. The lamp is on a length of flex cord and he twists it to in front of her and shines it down. Bill returns to his chair.

But the moment has also given him a chance to take a close look at her breasts. His first impression is that they aren't all that remarkable. They're round yes, and there is an uplift, but from how the kid talked, he half expected to see a marvel. Still, breasts are breasts, and every pair is different. Settling into his sketching, Bill is going to enjoy this.

And it pleases him that the girl seems comfortable. When their eyes meet, she even smiles, admitting the strangeness of what is happening. It helps Bill loosen up further.

The real difference is the guy, however. He has started becoming excited again and Bill is reminded of his gesturing and tracing in the air the first time they met. The kid moves to in front of the woman, then hurries to twist her slightly to the side. Again, he steps in front of her and scrutinizes. "The angle is everything, there just has to be that feel." Moving to her and pulling back her shoulders and having her sit up straight, Bill is reminded of the comical stereotype of a fanatical painter—all the kid needs is a goatee and an off-kilter beret.

The girl doesn't seem to mind. There is the feeling that with the kid hovering over her, she is enjoying the attention. When the kid stands back looking at her, she registers his gaze with an absorbing grin.

And suddenly Bill gets an idea of what the kid wants. He wants her turned a little at the waist so there is an off-center view, yet still a full frontal. That way the breasts will be accented, and the far breast will be almost in profile.

"Exactly!" the kid exclaims, delighted that Bill is understanding.

Bill moves his chair to the side to make the angle even more pronounced.

From there the sketch comes easily. The near arm of the woman is brought back a little to cause a tension in the figure, and the other arm is brought a little forward to keep the balance. That bit of tension makes the difference. With the figure feathered above the elbows, the arms can be lowered without the rest of the arms getting in the way.

It is a good design. Bill is impressed. And the sketching causes a slight thrill in him, harkening back to art school days when so much could be new and impressive. It has been a while since he has done this kind of sketching.

When the rough sketch is complete, Bill allows the two of them to have a look. They take a long look. It causes a pang in him to realize they aren't as impressed with it as he is; the girl doesn't know what to think, and although the guy likes it, he says a couple of things can be improved. Mostly he wants Bill to show the protrusion of the nipple area more. Again, he says it is what gives Jan's breasts their distinction.

But Bill didn't notice any such distinction. His reaction is to think the protrusion might be an exaggeration of the kid's mind. But he decides to take another look. The girl strikes the pose.

And there it is, he does see it! It's a surprise to him, and he is left wondering if he just missed it or maybe the breasts changed—he did work on them at the start of the sketch, and it has been quite a while since he really looked. Now there is a fullness to the nipple area, yes, a protrusion; as if the whole areola area is extended further—a separate pink-brown grape. It gives her body a fuller and more voluptuous feel. The only other thing Bill can think of is the kid pushing back her shoulders and having her sit up straight caused the difference, but the sketch hardly started then. Or maybe the girl is just reacting to the attention.

Tracing her breasts now, they seem very different. Bill is intrigued.

When the revision is done, the kid is pleased. "So you think you can get that in a tattoo?" he asks excited.

A lot of the lines will disappear but the basic outline should stay the same.

"You think you can get that feel?"

Bill grimaces. He can't be sure he knows exactly what the kid is talking about.

"I mean the fullness of her."

Again, Bill can't be completely sure. Fullness is a very subjective word.

The two of them look closely at the woman. Hearing herself talked about and being scrutinized has caused her to blush, yet it hasn't diminished her. The attention is more absorbed and radiated.

"Just the magnitude!" the kid ejects suddenly.

Bill finds himself nodding his head. Yes, he never would have put it that way but yes, a magnitude; a kind of potency.

As soon as he is convinced Bill understands, and in an outburst punctuated by his fists being raised near his head, the kid agrees to have the tattoo done. "Let's go for it!"

But Bill finds himself bracing against the kid's excite-ment—he hasn't agreed to anything. This is still an iffy proposition. Who's running this show? "Hold on a minute," he finds himself saying, as he rubs his chin and takes a moment to think.

The kid's expression is one of surprise. "It can be done can't it?"

Yes, it can be done, that's not the question.

"Hey you're the best," the kid states.

Bill is glad he thinks so. But this is something he has to be sure about. This has to be on his terms. Bill is on a threshold.

But what can he do? The momentum of everything so far has been to go forward, and he can't think of a good reason to stop. The bottom line is he does think he can do it. But it will be a challenge.

"Alright," he finally agrees. "I'm in."

An excitement breaks loose between them. The two of them are grinning, and Bill has to smile himself.

Bill then leads them back to his studio space and begins setting up.

"So how much you want for it?" the kid suddenly asks.

The question of price brings everything back to earth. Bill finds himself regretting the issue. It is also a detail he overlooked, and he is suddenly unsure what to charge and that bothers him more—it occurs to him that if he charges what the tattoo is really worth the kid might not have enough. It could be a way to get out of it, but now that Bill has decided to do it, he wants to go ahead.

"Eighty bucks."

It is agreed. Okay, this is going to happen. Bill sets about arranging the room.

The initial problem is that he will need another chair and quickly gets one from his office. It has occurred to him that he doesn't absolutely need the woman to pose for him anymore and she could put her shirt back on, but he wants her to stay posed for reference and inspiration. He sets her up in full view, sitting just off the side from where the kid's shoulder will be. Then there is the needle and pigment to get ready.

Another detail comes to him, and again there is a twinge of embarrassment—is he getting ahead of himself? He doesn't even know where the kid wants this thing. He could wait to see what part of his body gets turned toward the needle, but that won't be exact enough.

"So where do you want this?"

The kid answers directly. "On my stomach."

Woa! "On your stomach?" Bill cringes. It is the final crown on what has become an incredulous situation.

"Yeah, right here." In one motion the kid strips off his shirt and with his finger circles an area to the side of his navel.

Bill struggles not to react. Where the kid has circled is absolutely the most sensitive place on the body; there is going to be some pain. But he feels it wouldn't stop the kid anyway, so he decides not to worry him. "Okay, you're the wild man."

With everything set, they are ready to get started. The kid sits in the chair and Bill situates him sliding down a little, with his legs spread so Bill can move in and lean over his stomach. After he sits down, Bill decides he wants the girl more directly over the kid's shoulder and makes the adjustment. With the new arrangement, he is ready to begin.

With the whine of the needle, Bill gets himself focused— he had better; this operation could use both luck and a prayer. Inside him there is still a nagging uneasiness.

With the needle, he circles over the area of the stomach,

trying to feel for a place to start. He looks at the sketch pad propped up to his side on the tray of needles and pigment. He looks at the woman holding the pose. Again, there comes a feeling of absurdity—Geezuz.

His decision is to start at the base of the torso and make the sweeping line of the figure upward. He only wants to trace the roughest outline, very lightly.

When the needle touches skin, the kid's stomach muscles flinch. "Easy does it now," Bill cajoles. "Stay relaxed."

The kid promises, but as Bill starts again, he knows it won't be easy. To take the kid's mind off what is happening, Bill decides to talk to him. He has become curious enough about him anyway.

"So what's your name?" he asks, suddenly aware he doesn't even know the kid's name.

"Dan."

Dan. Hmm. Dan and Jan. Bill almost smiles, then he almost asks if their friends tease them about their names being so similar, but of course they do, so he doesn't bother.

"So what do you do, Dan?"

The kid hesitates. "Well, I work in a warehouse...but what I really do is play guitar."

There's something Bill can latch onto. "Oh yeah, in a band?"

"Yeah we got a band."

Bill's next inclination is to ask if they are any good, but of course there is no way to tell. From there, he almost asks what music the kid is into but doubts he would recognize any of it anyway.

"That's why I want this tattoo," Dan starts again. There

is that tone of earnestness in his voice that has come to be familiar. "For when I play."

That sounds reasonable enough. "For inspiration, huh?"

"Yeah," Dan says, pleased Bill understands. "I want her with me."

The last words don't quite reach Bill, as he has suddenly become absorbed in the detail of what he is doing. Yet through the whine of the needle and the sweeping out of the line, the explanation along with everything he has been feeling about the kid continues to gather, and then after another moment the whole thing hits him; he understands why the kid is so intent on having this tattoo, and why he wants it where he wants it and what it all means to him. Yeah, it's where his woman lives, where his music comes from. Bill should know he has music of his own, and a couple of women have made him feel that way.

The realization continues to expand until it includes everything he has come to feel about these two kids. They're trying to reach for something; they're trying to make some-thing real for themselves. To confirm the realization Bill lifts his head and looks around, and it's all there before him; the room seems to glow with an intensity. He feels it in the woman poised and proud, with her shoulders back and her breasts pert and swollen, offering all she is to the moment. He feels it in the stomach muscles beneath his hand, strug-gling not to spasm.

And where is he? In the middle of it all. How else can he view his life? Suddenly, Bill feels his own involvement—he's not just decorating a body anymore; this is important, it has to mean something.

Bill focuses further, and the intensity takes him until he

feels himself on the verge of one of those rare moments when things truly happen. The tip of the needle has become the focal point. It's up to him. And he has felt this way before so he knows what to do. From deep inside, at the very core of him comes his voice: It's yours, you mother...grab it...take it home!

The moment lifts him and sweeps him forward. And suddenly it doesn't matter that these kids probably don't have a snowball's chance in hell; that the world will probably tear them apart and they might even learn to hate each other; that the kid might someday pay good money to have this thing taken off. It just doesn't matter. Because there is a chance, and the chance is also for him. For now only the moment matters and Bill wants to accomplish all of it. For himself yes, and whatever else it can be. And things do come together. There is that flow and magnitude. And maybe for the first time in his life, he truly understands those grandiose words that float back to him from his days of art study, when the female form was referred to as a symbol of life...the continuing of nature...birth...love... joy. He also feels his own life combine to become something more. He pushes hard to be included in that rarified space.

The whine of the needle is the only sound. Everything in the room is captured and absorbed. The figure of the woman comes together.

The whine finally ends. There is a full collapse. Bill leans back, the kid relaxes, and the girl falls from her pose.

When Bill doesn't continue, the kid sits up, and in the same motion is standing and turning and bending over to look at his stomach. The girl hurries forward. "Killer!" the kid erupts, pumping his fists with the girl hanging onto him trying to see. "Yeah killer!"

Bill remains motionless in his chair, not even looking at them.

"You fuckin' did it man!"

Yes, he did it.

"Killer!"

He goddamn did it good.

A grin begins to spread, and in a rush of excitement, Bill pushes himself to his feet. He is in it now. The three of them are in it together. They circle around each other, swept up in the exuberance.

Dan leans backward against the desk so Bill and the girl can examine the tattoo more closely. It does look good!

"You're gonna play a mean guitar."

"I'm gonna fuckin' wail!"

Dan shakes Bill's hand ecstatically, with his other arm around Jan, with her arms wrapped around him. Stripped to the waist, they are two healthy hunks of exuberant flesh with big, beaming smiles. In the momentum of what they are feeling together, Bill for an instant imagines the three of them stripping off their clothes and getting into it with each other. The moment has taken him that far.

But already there is the feeling that the moment has passed its crescendo, though they continue to shake their heads and smile. Bill wants to take another look at the tattoo. Damn! It just has that feel.

Finally, Jan turns her back and puts on her shirt. Dan says if it wasn't for being cool outside, he wouldn't think of putting his shirt on, but finally does. To finish their dressing, they put on their jackets. Bill begins giving instructions about the care and healing process of the tattoo.

They linger a while, then one by one file out of the office. Together they walk to the front of the shop. It gives Bill an uneasy feeling of separateness when he walks behind the counter to the cash register, but what can he do? The kid is quick to get out his money and hands him two fifties.

"No change man."

Bill gives a quick nod of gratitude. "Thank you sir."

And in the meeting of their eyes there is a communication. It comes from the kid as he smiles warmly and gives a quick nod of his own. "'Preciate it man." Bill understands it as the kid knowing what he did for him and saying how much it meant.

As the two of them turn to leave with their arms around each other, Bill is again hit with a spasm of wanting the moment to continue. Go have a drink? Check out some music? But he is sure they are looking forward to the night ahead. Power to them. Walking with them to the front door Bill unlocks it. Before they leave they all give last smiles, quick nods and waves. Have a good one.

After closing the door, Bill walks back to the register. He finds himself placing his hands on either side of it, then leaning forward, he lowers his head. Well, that was sure something. When he straightens up, he is still amazed.

The absence of the two kids is felt, yet alone Bill finds himself filled with a unique clarity—a lightness of himself more than any new awareness.

He wants the feeling to continue. Bill does a quick job of closing the shop; all the money is his so that isn't a problem. After taking care of the lights and turning on the phone-answering machine, he grabs his buckskin jacket and walks out the door.

It is nearly dark now with just the last tinges of whitish blue in the sky near the horizon. Bill opens himself to a further peace, a matching of both inside and outside. Even the cool air feels good. Walking to his truck, there is the feeling the ol' beast is ready to charge down the street.

But getting in his truck, he is faced with a decision. Suddenly, the thought of spending another night at The Big Barrel jars him. Sitting with the same people, running the same ol' talk around, chasing after the same ol' stories. Bill just isn't into it. Not tonight, not after all that has happened. He has a feeling to protect, and he wants to savor it. Thinking about going to The Big Barrel has also given him a glimpse of himself and he shakes his head: Getting to be a boring old ex-hippie.

And it doesn't mean he's not going to do some drinking, and it doesn't mean he might not get a little drunk. And he'll surely be looking for something a little wild, but it won't be at The Big Barrel.

With the decision final, a flash of the ecstasy returns. He has caught a wave and only wants to ride it. Pulling out of the parking lot, he presses the accelerator, giving the truck a steady stream and it responds. Just who the hell knows? He might even meet someone. Just who the hell knows? Reaching the curve, he takes it nice and steady, then points the truck toward the other side of town.

What Worlds Exist
Between Is and Isn't

Working the oil fields in western Oklahoma, I was instructed by a foreman on the proper construction of a burn pile. He told me the way to tell the fire was hot enough was when the top of the flames curled as if trying to escape their own momentum. Only then would the fire be hot enough to consume everything at its core. As the foreman gave instruction, his tone was of relaying finer details gained from years of experience. I believed I knew what he meant, having seen news footage of raging house fires and forest fires where flames curled as had been described. I built a pile of debris by machine, first with smaller limbs and branches before adding larger trunks and root stumps. The fire burned well into the night.

I must have been watching public television because PBS was the only channel available to me that would have featured such a documentary. The program chronicled the legacy of an extended family of demolition experts, world-renowned for their feats of taking down large buildings even in crowded urban settings, surrounded by similar great buildings without damaging the adjacent structures in the least. The film footage was amazing. At a given moment, a massive building would show puffs of detonation at its base, then collapse straight down on itself and remain contained to its footprint. The family had been doing this for decades and was widely regarded as the greatest. A fascinating picture emerged through interviews, in-depth explanation of the engineering involved, the process of calculations, the strategy of blast patterns and the positioning of charges.

The family patriarchs were steely serious and determined men, projecting strength and focus. At one point, the grandson or great-grandson, was featured as the youngest member of the lineage and the one to eventually take over the business. He appeared to be in his late twenties, of solid size and shape with an open, expressive and youthful face. When he talked about his career path, an exuberance bubbled forth; his work was also his pleasure. When asked about his ambitions, he quickly stated, staring directly into the camera, that his greatest goal was to take down a skyscraper with a firecracker. The outrageousness of his statement didn't seem to register. There was no sense of hyperbole or dramatic bluster. His attitude was matter-of-fact, as if all it would take was the continuing development of his skills; his commitment to extending the effect of minimal effort producing maximum gain would reach into the realm of magic.

My interest in T'ai Chi Ch'uan began as a need to move my body. In the attic of the house where I lived, I made sweeping motions of my hands and arms coordinated with broad circular steps and the turning of my waist, imitating the graceful movements I must have seen on television or in the movies. Shortly after expressing my interest to a therapist I had been doing work with, she gave me the names and numbers of a few T'ai Chi teachers from her network. After a couple of phone calls, I contacted a soft-spoken but engaging woman who communicated the concepts and focus of T'ai Chi. Most importantly, she mentioned that she started a new class twice a year and the next class happened to begin the following week.

I walked into an auditorium filled with maybe fifty enthused people. When class started, it was directed to movements of the body. The teacher was a petite Asian woman who, during times of pause, touched on the background and principles of Tai Chi as an ancient Chinese art of movement and meditation. The form we would study was a series of postures strung together by the continuous ebb and flow of chi, internal energy. The cultivation of chi led to health and well-being. The form itself took nine months to complete.

By the end of that first class, I felt strongly that I would be there quite a while. I was a young man just past thirty, hungry for greater meaning in life and anxious to pursue a spiritual path. Spirituality for me could be summed up in a quote I recollected, as the understanding that "all religious impulse is an attempt to reconcile the finite with the infinite." As for a practice to pursue, I understood that a vine needed a wall to grow against. The only advice I remember regarding the choice of a spiritual path was to select one that had deep roots, had withstood the test of time, had the opportunity to refine itself through study and scrutiny, and wasn't subject to the whims of fad and fashion.

T'ai Chi Ch'uan's roots were in Taoism, the ancient Chinese philosophy seeking insight into the nature of reality through observing the natural world and aligning oneself in balance and harmony with the flow of the universe. The focus was on a holistic approach to mind, body, spirit, and because of those interconnections, working with the body to work on what you could see was a way of working on what you couldn't see. The most important thing was to relax. By letting tension and discord fall away, the body became connected, and through simple movement, cultivated the exchange of yin and yang—the interdependent yet complementary forces of change, of energy, the irreducible essence of everything.

My teacher, Carol Yamasaki, was a direct student of Professor Cheng Man-ch'ing, a world-renowned master of T'ai Chi Ch'uan and the originator of our modified form. The Professor had fled China with Chiang Kai-shek during the Cultural Revolution in 1949 and settled in Taiwan, where he started his school before traveling to New York City, where he was invited to establish a second school. He was known as the master of five excellences, which, besides T'ai Chi Ch'uan included painting, calligraphy, poetry, and Chinese medicine. Of those, he believed the study of T'ai Chi to be most beneficial to mankind. My teacher, Carol, had studied with the professor for several years before moving back to her hometown in the Detroit area and starting her own school.

One of my teacher's unique and remarkable qualities, which I came to only fully appreciate years later as testament to her humility and continuing desire to learn, was her willingness to open her school to other ideas and influences. While most teachers starting a school positioned themselves as the authority from which most ideas flowed, Carol invited other practitioners to come to our school and teach and hold workshops. Each brought decades of experience. Our school became a hub for teachers from both the East and West coasts, where our lineage was most prominent, and from places as far away as Taiwan.

I was part of a great lineage. I felt the power of deep study and had found direction for my greatest intrigue. All my young man's hunger for knowledge and connection poured into my practice. Attending class twice a week wasn't enough, so I organized an additional class with fellow students and rented a dance studio. Including my personal workouts, I practiced T'ai Chi more than ten hours a week.

T'ai Chi Ch'uan also had a martial arts component to the practice I wasn't initially aware of. It referenced the Ch'uan in T'ai Chi Ch'uan, and the full translation of the art into English as "Supreme Ultimate Boxing." T'ai Chi Ch'uan was a soft martial art that focused on the soft overcoming the hard through the power of yielding. It cultivated investing in loss, the power of not doing, the emphasis on neutralizing an opponent by receiving and returning energy, to giving oneself over to follow others through listening and connection. The spiritual focus was learning to experience oneself in relation to another. "Push-hands", as the martial format of our practice, was the other side of the coin from learning and studying the open-hand form. Its study took up the second half of our class time together.

Due to my teacher's prominence in the T'ai Chi Ch'uan network, I was able to make contact with the most accomplished living martial arts practitioners of our lineage, Mr. Liu Hsin and Benjamin Pang Jeng Lo. They were two of the Professor's first students in Taiwan and were most responsible for carrying on the great tradition. During my experience, Mr.Liu was in his early eighties, Ben Lo a decade or so younger. Between them, they had over a hundred years of practice and study. What struck me most after spending time with each of them was their remarkable differences. It hardly seemed possible that they had come from the same teacher, although they had both been classmates as young men and remained compatriots throughout their lives. Ben Lo was direct and physical, a definite man of action, while Mr. Liu was scholarly, serene. But what was most baffling was the differences in their approach to teaching. Ben Lo focused on each individual posture of the form, emphasizing the need for correctness and precision, so that the body could be an open vessel to gather and expand chi. Mr. Liu focused on the flow of energy itself being connected and continuous throughout the body's changes. I could not see any overlap between the two great men. I was reminded of the Zen saying, "There are many paths to the top of Mt. Fuji." Their differences were best explained by the Professor himself when he was to have said that in the study of T'ai Chi Ch'uan, Ben Lo received "yang", the great active force of extending, maybe best understood as male energy and the energy of the sun, as one dynamic of the great primordial life force. Mr. Liu received the other seemingly opposing but complementary force of "yin", best expressed as feminine energy, receiving and reflective, passive, like the moon. The Professor tailored his teaching to the character of each student. Their differences were testament to the great expanse of T'ai Chi Ch'uan.

My first experiences were with Benjamin Pang Jeng Lo. For a period of my study, he visited our school twice a year to hold a weekend workshop. Ben Lo led his own school in San Francisco and was head of what was considered the West Coast branch of our lineage. As one of Professor's senior students, Ben had great authority, but his demeanor was decidedly casual. Ben Lo was modest in stature, slightly muscular, always dressed in American-style jeans featuring a rather large belt buckle, and long-sleeved button-down cotton flannel shirt. He appeared relaxed and could be open and engaging, but there was an intensity about him: he was supremely confident, direct and powerful. I had the feeling of someone capable of crushing through rock; I thought of him as a military man and could easily imagine him at the head of a group of soldiers leading a charge into battle.

Ben Lo's classes could be tough and even grueling. His whole focus was to achieve. The position of the body had to be precise. He had little sympathy for inability. He led us through the series of postures that made up the form one at a time, with each posture being held as he talked through the different principles of T'ai Chi that needed to be accounted for as he walked down the rows of students and took time to correct the positions of the hands and feet and body of each. Consequently, each posture could be held for several minutes. The requirement for each posture was to focus on one leg or the other. Holding a posture wasn't a matter of muscle and bone but of release and opening, an engagement with the ground that naturally gathered energy before expanding up through the body to the top of the head and out to the fingertips. After a period of standing, the legs began to burn. Ben's adage was "No burn, no earn." Any hope of progress demanded the full focus of doing it right. A correction class would go on for more than an hour. At the end, people could be gasping. In my more resisting moments, I complained to myself that Ben Lo had a touch of the sadist. But it was understood that his method reflected his own instruction from the professor and his strong desire for people to receive the benefits of the great art he so valued. At the end of a day of class, I remember driving home and having to lift my leg by my pants to move my foot between the gas pedal and the brake. After a Ben Lo workshop, my legs always took a day or so to recover.

Ben Lo was a martial arts master. His reputation was for taking on all challengers. The power of his internal energy was legendary. In his engagement with others, he didn't hold back and felt that once the chi was activated, it had a power of its own that was obligated to be fulfilled. If an opponent could not yield and the energy found them, it was their fault. Whoever received the discharge as a result could be in for a devastating blast. In his younger days, there were stories of people getting hurt. Only as he got older did Ben Lo mellow. As the story was told, after having his first child and holding the newborn in his arms, he experienced true helplessness and vulnerability, which softened his approach and attitude toward his opponents. When I knew him, he could be fierce but also kind and gentle.

During class breaks, Ben Lo enjoyed telling stories,

mostly about his involvement with his teacher, Professor Chen Men Cheng. We often encouraged him because it meant less time for posturing and burning our legs. A story I heard more than once was that as a young student, Ben decided to test his teacher to see for himself if the Professor was indeed deserving of all the time and effort he was investing. He approached from behind and, without the Professor knowing, attacked him. The next thing Ben knew, he was sliding down a wall with blood coming from his mouth. The Professor rushed to him, shocked and concerned. "What did you do? Why did you do that?" After all the years that had passed, Ben Lo's eyes widened in amazement when he told the story. "It was like touching the power!" he said in his stilted English, referring to what it must feel like to touch electricity.

My best experience with Ben Lo was when I had the chance to do push-hands with him. As a serious student who had at least proved a good level of interest in the art, I believe he thought me worthy of a lesson. A group of class-mates gathered several steps behind, as was customary, in case someone needed to be caught. Ben Lo and I came together, our arms and hands connecting in the slow-moving exchange of the push-hands form. At one point, I had the impression of my mind remaining with my hands where they lightly touched Ben Lo on his extended forearm, while my body had separated to be a great distance across the room.

My great interest in T'ai Chi Ch'uan led me to travel to Taipei, Taiwan, to study with Mr. Liu Hsin. For him to accept me required a letter of recommendation from my teacher. By then, I had been studying for six years. I planned to study with Mr. Liu for two years. I was scheduled to go with a classmate, who became ill just before we left, so I continued alone. The trip was brutal. Finding my way to where I was to stay, daunting. The language barrier, almost insurmountable. It took every effort to arrive at the studio on the designated day and time.

A Westerner coming to study with Mr. Liu wasn't uncommon, and after a brief acknowledgment of my arrival, I simply fell in line with the dozen or so other students to begin class. Mr. Liu, for me, was the epitome of Ta'i Chi Ch'uan accomplishment and possibility. While Ben Lo equally shared the highest level of stature and respect amongst our lineage, from everything I heard, I felt more aligned with Mr. Liu's approach. Mr. Liu was a practicing Buddhist and said to meditate for hours daily. He was also married, his wife attended class, he had raised children, worked a government job for a career. Mr. Liu for many years, headed Professor's large school in Taipei but had since retired to teach a few students privately.

Mr. Liu dressed in the traditional Chinese garb of a thin cotton blouse and maybe a loose jacket over wide, light-cotton, baggy pants. He was lean and lanky, wore glasses, was quick to smile, and radiated calm and a clear focus. Mr. Liu had the demeanor of a wise sage, and I could easily imagine him retreated to a mountaintop. After spending time with him, I remember describing being in his presence as being available to the sun in the first days of spring, when you couldn't take off enough clothes and expose your skin to the warmth and radiance. I became so intrigued with him that after learning the route he traveled to walk through the busy streets back to where he lived, I would wait inside a bakery along the way to watch him walk past.

T'ai Chi Ch'uan had both a great literary and oral tradition, and Mr. Liu was committed to communicating everything that intrigued him. He spoke minimal English but always had an interpreter available. A great exuberance rose as he expounded; his hands would flash around his eyes, his face beaming enthusiastically. He used a chalkboard to diagram and demonstrate. I was free to ask questions, though I often felt I didn't know enough to know what to ask, so my initiative was to listen attentively and take copious notes.

Mr. Liu's studio was on top of a three-story building with a free-standing roof. Two of the sides along the perimeter were walls lined vertically with woven tatami mats intended to cushion a student if they were being discharged in the process of doing push-hands. Mr. Liu's focus on the study of T'ai Chi Ch'uan was the cultivation of internal energy through continuous movement and the constant flow of exchange between yin and yang, the two polarities of interplay that combined to become one. Tai Chi was an art of reduction, of returning after a life of being divided and separated to the energy of primordial power. By relaxing and connecting, the gates of the body opened and the chi freely circulated, like silk being pulled from a cocoon. A story that most demonstrated an essential focus of T'ai Chi was when, as a student, Mr. Liu went to deliver a message to the Professor, and so as not to disturb him, stood outside the partially opened door and waited. The Professor was at a lectern, turning the pages of a manuscript, he read while shifting from one leg to another. When the Professor noticed Mr. Liu, he beckoned him in, and in reference to his movement, he said that what he was doing was all there was to T'ai Chi. T'ai Chi was simple but not easy. The challenge was to get the body out of the way.

Class with Mr. Liu was twice a week, leaving me plenty of time for myself. I had come to Taipei for only one thing, and after making inquiries, I became connected with other teachers of my lineage who held classes throughout the city. I also had my personal workouts. If each day were divided into two possible morning and afternoon workout periods, of the fourteen weekly opportunities, I practiced thirteen, giving myself Sunday afternoon off.

Mr. Liu himself was a profound martial artist who focused on the power of yielding and receiving to neutralize an opponent and gather energy to be expressed in the power of discharge. His reputation was of being almost ethereal. People engaging with Mr. Liu said it was like entering a fog: surrounded, you lost all sense of reference and were trapped to yourself while not being able to find Mr. Liu anywhere. Push-hands students much more proficient than I said they wouldn't touch Mr. Liu in a true martial arts encounter for any amount of money. The most senior student of Ben Lo's, who after much effort, gained a brief push-hands lesson with Mr. Liu, described the experience as touching steel wrapped in cotton.

After four months of studying with Mr. Liu, I was forced to leave the country due to changes in the visa requirements. Before I left, I made sure Mr. Liu knew I would be going, so I was available if he wanted to give any personal instruction. Sure enough, he called me over and, through the interpreter, asked me to do the simplest shifting from one leg to the other while coordinating the movements of my arms and hands in what is known as the brush-knee sequence. Mr. Liu was seated in front of me. After a few repetitions, he looked at me with a smile and said, through translation. "You have worked very hard but have solved nothing." He told me to try over the weekend before returning for my final class. He watched again but noticed no improvement.

At that time, I had a serious talk with myself and gave myself permission to quit the practice. Learning T'ai Chi Ch'uan was far beyond anything I imagined. Throughout my life, anything I set my mind to accomplish, I was able, after a period of effort, to at least show some tangible results. With T'ai Chi, the more I tried, the further away I seemed to get. I remembered Ben Lo saying it took two lifetimes to learn T'ai Chi. But it was also fascinating and exhilarating and offered true insight into the nature of energy and how the world worked. T'ai Chi was worthy of a life. After spending time with Mr. Liu, I felt that I was at least outside the room, and although I couldn't gain entrance, by pressing my face against the glass, I could see what was inside. I returned to the States and practiced diligently for four years before returning to Taipei. Again, I had the chance to be in front of Mr. Liu and shift from one leg to the other, shoulder-width apart, while coordinating my hands and arms in the sequence of brush-knee. Mr. Liu watched closely before, with a wry grin, offering his assessment. Even the translator smiled. "Your energy is like swamp water, only good for breeding mosquitoes." I went home and studied for another few years before coming back.

My greatest singular lesson from Mr. Liu happened in push-hands. It was my turn to push with him in class. I faced Mr. Liu with my back to the wall of tatami mats. Mr. Liu and I came together to lightly touch and combine our energies in the sequence of receiving and returning, the exchange of yin and yang. It wasn't that I couldn't feel Mr. Liu, I could sense the surface of him, though it only reflected my position. It was like touching an empty coat. Yet Mr. Liu's awareness had absorbed and permeated my body; I felt completely dominated. At one point, Mr. Liu took advantage of an opening I provided and gently moved into the space and trapped me into something stuck and solid. I should have surrendered to the inevitable discharge, but at that final moment, I made the slightest adjustment of my body. At that most intense moment before push, with the outcome determined, when in every other martial exchange I had encountered, my partner would be focused on the position of their own body to have the best chance for a successful discharge, Mr. Liu's reaction to my slightest movement was to yield completely, to give himself over to receiving, to absorb and accommodate my movement and energy throughout his entire body. Mr. Liu's great ability was pure response, beyond anything of interest or intent; he made himself available to capture any energy available. In a true martial arts setting, my only recourse for survival would have been to turn around and run.

While camping in a wilderness area in Washington State with the woman who would become my wife, we watched three lights converge in the sky on a starry night and hover suspended for several moments before racing off in different directions. "What the hell?" we echoed to each other in amazement. Eventually, we returned to sitting at the campfire and staring into the flames. We talked about things weird and crazy, and delved deeper into conversation about what it was like living in a world with so much we would never understand.

One of my greatest pleasures is taking a large tract of unfamiliar land and, by following patterns of terrain and the paths of animals, reducing the expanse to the size of a heart that can be pierced by an arrow.

In a distant country, a hundred and eighty mass graves were discovered containing the bodies of three hundred thousand victims.

At the highest point on Earth are found the fossils of ancient sea creatures.

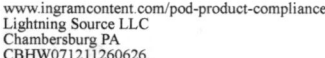